ARCADIA'S CHILDREN 3: PUSHLEY'S ESCAPE

A sequel to Arcadia's Children 2:
The Fyfield Plantation

By

Andrew R. Williams

REVIEWS

Arcadia's Children 3: Pushley's Escape – Reviewed By Piaras O Cionnaoith For Emerald Book Reviews

Arcadia's Children 3 Pushley's Escape... the adventure continues!

Forty-some years ago my uncle gave me a science fiction anthology. It was a thick red hardback that I read from cover to cover. It inspired a lifelong love of the genre. The stories in that book made me think outside the box. They filled me with awe for the imagination it took to write them. That book still remains in my collection today. The title is OMNIBUS OF SCIENCE FICTION, edited by Groff Conklin, a well-known and prolific editor of the genre. It was published in 1952, the Golden Age of Science Fiction. It's a substantial volume, 562 pages, with 43 stories divided into sections relating to a common theme. Some stories are fun, some are thought-provoking, and some are adventurous. I love them all.

Arcadia's Children 3: Pushley's Escape by Andrew R. Williams is the third instalment in the Arcadia's Children series. The author weaves another well-crafted sci-fi fantasy that will grab readers and hurl them far beyond the boundaries of our limited world. The threads of storytelling are expertly woven in this highly imaginative science fiction tale that guarantees the attention of the reader. Skilfully constructed, this fantasy will have you turning the pages from beginning to end. The imagery in the writing style makes you feel like you are right there in the story.

As with the previous two books in this series, ARCADIA'S CHILDREN: SAMANTHA'S REVENGE and ARCADIA'S CHILDREN 2: THE FYFIELD PLANTATION, the main characters remain the same; Mick Tarmy, Claire Hyndman and Nonie Tomio.

The author introduces us to this instalment with the following synopsis:

Ed Pushley is an archaeologist, but his mind has been taken over by a spettro that Mick Tarmy dubbed as Irrelevant. (My name is Irrelevant, Mr. Tarmy.) Irrelevant and Pushley are now one. Following Irrelevant's death their minds have fused. Kept captive by Alton Mygael, Pushley frantically tries to find a means of escape. Damaging his isolation helmet during a moment of frustration, Pushley realizes that with perseverance he can remove it, and can use Irrelevant's immense psychic powers to gain his freedom. Once he does, what will he do to Mick Tarmy and his team? Pushley is intent on revenge.'

I enjoyed the story, the continued character development, and dialogue. There were plenty of twists and turns that I didn't see coming and that added to the book's magic. When I stopped reading to work, I found myself wondering what happened in the book, and replaying parts of the novel in my head to see if I could figure more out. It has been a while since I enjoyed a book this much. It's a first-class sci-fi fantasy with perfect pacing.

I'm a big fan of science fiction, so this for me was a phenomenal read. For sci-fi fans looking for an interesting, three-dimensional and stimulating read, this would be a great find. I'm giving nothing further away here. And this, I hope, will only add to the mystery and enjoyment for the reader.

I'll be looking forward to reading more from Andrew R. Williams in the future. A well-deserved five stars from me.

Arcadia's Children 3: Pushley's Escape – reviewed by Sherin for Goodreads

5 Stars!

Just the sequel I have been waiting for! As always, the storytelling is great, and the realm painted in this book feeds our imagination and the visual imagery that comes to life with the way the book is written...a treat that was worth the wait!

A very interesting and exciting continuation of this series where we get to see the action and adventure of our favourite characters all over again. I loved the action scenes, the way Pushley was handled by Tarmy and the joint effort by his team including Claire.

This riveting series is only getting better and I can't wait to read what's next for Arcadia. After reading the final bit of update on Tarmy and his team and even more excited to read where this ride takes us next.

Dedication:
To Tom, Beryl, Bert, Peggy and Colin: gone but not forgotten.

THE AUTHOR

By day mild mannered Andrew R. Williams is a chartered surveyor.... but after twilight falls, he snatches up his pen and lets the writing take control. The Arcadia's Children series are sci-fi thrillers which pour out of Andrew on only the coldest and darkest of nights. When he isn't writing, or chartered surveying, Andrew spends time with his wife Geraldine, staring up at the stars, and plotting eventual world domination. Don't let that calm demeanour and easy smile fool you, oh no!

Other Books By Andrew R Williams:

Science Fiction
Arcadia's Children (Samantha's Revenge)
ISBN 978-1- 61309-710-6 (also in ebook)

Arcadia's Children 2: The Fyfield Plantation
ISBN 978-1- 61309-630-7 (also in ebook)

Novel (Action Thriller)
Jim's Revenge: ISBN ISBN-10: 1916312411

ISBN-13: 978-1916312418

Technical Books

Technical Domestic Building Surveys
ISBN 0 419 178000 7 (also in ebook)

Spons Practical Guide to Alterations and Extension
ISBN 10: 0-415-43426-2 (also in ebook)

Web Links:
https://www.amazon.co.uk/Andrew-R.-Williams/e/ B001HPK7KK

https://www.arcadiaschildren.com/

http://www.authorsden.com/andrewrwilliams

Extract From Arcadian Archaeology

Arcadia

Arcadia is the third planet in the Salus System. As it is in a Goldilocks zone, the world is an Earth-type.

Arden

Arden is Arcadia's main moon, primarily owned by the Minton Mining Company.

First Empire Colonisation of Arcadia/Rediscovery

Although the actual facts will probably never be known, it is generally accepted that Arcadia was colonised partway through the First Empire Period. However, the colonisation was far from planned. As The Wreck is still in orbit around Arcadia and has been the subject of intense scientific investigation, it is generally thought that the colonisation of Arcadia was accidental and that the passengers and crew of the Empress of Incognita were marooned.

Since its rediscovery, Arcadia has been declared a POSSI (Planet of Special Scientific Interest) and colonisation has been restricted. The reason for this is that Arcadia is an Earth-type planet and has developed life forms of its own. The native human population, the Ab are descendants of the starship survivors. They are not allowed to leave Arcadia to prevent the transfer of potentially dangerous pathogens from Arcadia to the other colonies in the Salus System. As another precaution, access to Arcadia is restricted to archaeological teams and palaeontologists who are quarantined (usually on Arden) upon their return from Arcadia.

The Wreck

Although badly damaged, The Wreck is still subjected to scrutiny. It has also become a major tourist attraction. Since teleportation systems were installed, over two million tourists per annum visit The Wreck.

Character Details From Arcadia's Children: Samantha's Revenge And Arcadia's Children 2: The Fyfield Plantation.

Mick Tarmy - an ex-Ardenese police officer blackmailed into going to Arcadia by Samantha and becoming Mick Tarleton, a notorious war criminal.

Amanda Tarmy - Mick Tarmy's daughter

Hen Jameson - Arden's former Chief of Civil police
Ord Morley, Vlad Pen and Ben Lieges - Police officers who used to work with Mick Tarmy

Alain Pen - Vlad Pen's son.

Claire Hyndman/Zia Warmers - Sent to Arcadia as Mick Tarmy's backup.

Alex - a TK5 - An ex-military patrol/attack droid; Claire Hyndman's invisible friend.

Nonie Tomio, Lascaux Kurgan and Chou Lan - archaeologists who worked with Claire Hyndman at Fort Saunders and Cittavecchia.

Alton Mygael (Oddface) - Former Director of Minton Mining Company Security.

Klaien Mygael - Alton Mygael's life partner.

Samantha - an Ingermann-Verex R9054 humanoid; Deputy Director of Minton Mining Company Security.

Mih Valanson - a scientific technician, formerly worked for Samantha - allowed Alex to escape.

Allus Wren - formerly a Senior Group Leader working for Samantha, now working for Alton Mygael.

Henry - a spettro prisoner who is forced into working for Samantha

Hal Warmers - Zia Warmers' partner, a black-marketeer and terrorist.

The Great Ones - a hostile Arcadian organisation, dedicated to the conquest of humanity.

Irrelevant - a spettro commander killed by an Arcadian plesiosaur. (See also Ed Pushley)

Ed Pushley - a senior archaeologist, now possessed by Irrelevant's soul.

Yalt - an Ab teleport worker forced into helping Ed Pushley.

Red Moxstroma and Bryn Rosslyn - Rescued by Mike Tarmy from the Fyfield Plantation.

The Great Ones' Army comprises:

Spettri (Plural) Spettro (Male) Spettra (Female) - Mutant humanoids.

Longjaw - a type of spettra, a mutant human, used by the Great Ones for general and military duties.

Arcadian wolves, Arcadian millipedes, Arcadian plesiosaurs.

A hyperlinked bubble appeared. Walter Verex said, "You might like to see this."

Samantha's image appeared in the bubble. The display panel near to the top of her conical body then enlarged; instead of displaying her regular arrogant face, the panel was showing the word, 'Retired'.

A moment later, a black-clad officer appeared and made an urgent request for assistance. Verex's image returned and said, "I promised to deactivate Samantha; I've done it."

Alton Mygael said, "This means we can return to Arden."

"It certainly does."

~*~

Yalt recognised Mih Valanson the moment he walked into the teleport centre; he was the man who'd shot him. Catching a glimpse of Yalt, Valanson looked surprised, confirming Yalt's thoughts. But instead of confronting one another, they both remained silent. It was if they'd come to an unspoken understanding; it was water under the bridge.

Alton Mygael glanced at Klaien, his life partner and said, "Once we arrive and I know everything is under control, I will contact you then everyone else will be able to teleport too."

"I don't want you to go back," Klaien said. "You know I think it's a trap. Walter Verex is lying to you; I don't believe him."

"Samantha is history," Alton Mygael replied, slight exasperation in his tone, "I have spoken to several board members who've confirmed that Samantha is defunct."

"Can't you see? It's a trap! They're all lying to you."

"No, they are not," Alton Mygael snapped. "I trust these people. Samantha's gone. I will have their support; they won't arrest me if I return. I *have* to go back; duty calls."

Mygael glanced at Wren and Philips. When they immediately came to attention, he said, "See, us Zadernaster boys stick together."

He walked towards the teleport bay. Klaien looked at Wren, "Do it!"

He hesitated.

"Do it!"

This time, Wren complied. Slipping his stun gun out of its holster, he shot Alton Mygael. As Yalt tried to run away, Mih Valanson grabbed hold of him and restrained him. Tam Philips moved in to assist and made sure he couldn't escape. Giving them both a wide-eyed look, Yalt said, "What's going on?"

Klaien walked over, "My partner wouldn't listen to reason. Don't worry; he's only stunned. Once he recovers, he won't even remember what happened."

Wren joined them, "We think he was about to teleport into a well-laid trap. So, we stopped him going."

When Yalt just stared at him open-mouthed, Wren spoke to Valanson. The other man handed him two cards; Wren put them into his shirt pocket and then slipped on a head camera. He then nodded at Yalt, "Come on then - time for you to teleport me to Arden."

Yalt objected, "Three of you are supposed to teleport."

Wren patted his pocket and then glanced at Valanson; "These two cards will make the teleport indicate its transporting three people; namely, Alton Mygael, Tam Philips and myself, but I'm the only one going."

"Have you got your return ticket? You might need it?" Klaien asked. Wren felt in his pocket for the boomerang device that Mih Valanson had manufactured for just that sort of eventuality.

After nodding, Wren stepped onto the teleport platform. As anticipated, the teleport confirmed it was transporting three people. Philips gave Yalt a nudge, "Do it."

Reluctantly, Yalt pressed a button. A moment later, Wren's body turned transparent and then disappeared from view.

Author's Note – If you have read, Arcadia's Children 2: The Fyfield Plantation, you may remember this chapter. I have included it as a link and extended it slightly.

CHAPTER ONE

THE RAID ON THE FYFIELD PLANTATION

G lancing towards the survivor tower, Wren said, "So, this is where you've been hiding your droid?"

"Droids," Mick Tarmy corrected. He'd barely spoken the word before two of the A10s emerged from the top of the tower and moved on an intercept course. As the A10's moved in and boxed his air-car, Tarmy added, "As well as Alex, the TK5, we also have four A10s designed for police enforcement duties."

Glancing out at the A10s, Wren said, "You never said you had other droids."

"You never asked," Tarmy replied nonchalantly.

"You just thought you'd keep it up your sleeve," Wren replied, a touch of acid in his tone.

"If I told you everything I know, you'd be as wise as I am," Tarmy countered. "I've learned that trusting people and droids can be a perilous fault."

"Life can be hard, and difficult if you don't trust anyone," Wren observed. He glanced out at the A10s again. "So, what's the story? Where did they come from?"

"Let's just call them spoils of war," Tarmy replied. "We captured them."

"Let me guess; from Stert Oryx?"

"Correct," Tarmy said. "Oryx tried to jump us when we were with the convoy on the Fyfield River. Alex has an enhanced interconnectivity system; when Oryx tried to use the A10's against us, Alex seduced them; they've been working for us ever since."

"Seduced them?"

"Took them over and made them work for us," Tarmy replied. "Alex has all sorts of special gismos incorporated into his systems."

"You do realise Arcadia has been declared a droid-free planet," Wren cautioned.

Tarmy grinned, "Is that so? Who enforces it?"

Wren shot him a hard look, and said, "Every time a new illegal colony pops up on Arcadia, the Interplanetary authorities launch a new intervention satellite."

"They are equipped with downward acting Mannheims designed to incapacitate droids," Wren replied. "If you blunder into one of the droid destroying Mannheims, your machines will fry and become useless junk."

"Thanks for the warning," Tarmy replied. "But I've been told we will be heading for a Mannheim free zone."

"If you're not careful, you could still run into trouble. If you parade these droids around too much, someone will probably report you to the authorities. Then interplanetary enforcement officers might come after you. They carry modern anti-droid weapons; you might end up having no droids and wind up in prison to boot."

"Once again, I'll bear that in mind," Tarmy replied. "I'll make sure we keep them hidden unless we need to use them."

Wren went quiet for a while and then said, "Presumably the A10s are useful; otherwise you would have kept them, would you?"

"The A10s don't have the punch Alex does, but they're interesting machines. They also make up for the TK5's only design flaw."

"Which is?"

"Alex, our TK5 doesn't have any secondary armament. With only a phaser, he has to avoid firing if he is likely to cause injury to his side. In contrast, the A10s have long-distance stun guns and various crowd dispersal devices. They can take down individuals at five hundred metres without killing them, which can be a handy attribute, in some cases."

"A handy attribute in some cases," Wren echoed. "What cases have you got in mind?"

Tarmy shrugged, "As I said before; I've learned that trusting people can be a perilous fault."

After a long silence, Wren said, "Why is it I get the impression you're sending me a coded message?"

"If I am, I hope you've received it loud and clear," Tarmy responded.

"The question is, why are you sending me the message?"

"It had occurred to me that Alton Mygael might have instructed you to force me to hand over Alex once the mission was complete," Tarmy replied. "If you try that one, the A10s will deal with you. One other point, if Alton Mygael tries to keep the others hostage in Awis Oasis I am willing to take the risk and send my droids into the Awis Mannheim. If Alex is right, droids can survive inside the Awis Mannheim as long as they don't remain under it for more than two hours. If Alton Mygael tries to keep my friends as hostages, I'll use my droids against him. Understood?"

"I can assure you he's given me no instruction to force you into parting with Alex," Wren replied. "In any case, Alton Mygael knows enough about military droids to realise they form a bond with their controller. If we attempted to take Alex, it's highly unlikely he'd obey our orders unless we knew how to reprogram him, which we don't."

When Tarmy remained silent, Wren added, "As far as I am concerned, once you've destroyed the Fyfield Plantation and hopefully rescued Anto Jaks, you're free to go."

"I'm glad we understand one another," Tarmy replied. "But it might be prudent to let Alton Mygael know the situation. I don't want any misunderstandings at a later date."

Wren nodded, "I'll make sure Alton Mygael gets your message loud and clear, and I'll make sure he heeds it."

"I also expect him to make sure that Walter Verex keeps his promises regarding my daughter and my former colleagues," Tarmy growled.

"I'm sure Verex is on the level," Wren replied. "He genuinely wants to destroy the Fyfield Plantation. He wants to make sure other people aren't affected like his grandson. It's become a personal vendetta. If you destroy the Fyfield Plantation, Verex will play ball."

"Glad to hear it," Tarmy said. "One more message for Alton Mygael. Once we've destroyed the plantation and hopefully brought Anto Jaks out alive, Claire, Nonie and everyone else will be flown out to the tower. I expect them to be here when we return, understood?"

Wren nodded and said, "Understood." He put a call into Alton Mygael.

Listening in to the conversation, Tarmy realised Mygael had agreed to everything he wanted.

Once his air-car was hovering alongside the tower, Chou Lan appeared at an opening and gave Tarmy a wave.

After manoeuvring, Tarmy landed the machine; glancing at Wren and Philips, he said, "You two stay in the air-car until I've talked things over with my people."

As Tarmy climbed out, both Chou Lan and Bryn Rosslyn came over and gave him a combined hug. "You're back."

Chou glanced into the air-car and saw Wren and Philips. "Where are the others?"

"Don't worry, I promise you they're all safe," he said. "Where's Alex?"

He barely asked the question before he felt Alex's invisible presence directly above him.

Glancing at Chou and Bryn, Tarmy said, "We all need to talk in private, including you Alex." He then began walking towards the opening in the cross wall. After checking no one could overhear, Tarmy said, "I have to go back to the Fyfield Valley."

"Why?"

Tarmy swiftly explained how he'd managed to organise his

daughter's escape from Arden. From there, he told them why her flight could be in danger.

"I still don't see why you have to go back," Bryn Rosslyn said.

"Blackmail, pure and simple," Tarmy said. "If I destroy the plantation, my daughter goes free. If I don't, she'll be returned to Arden and Samantha will send her back to prison, or worse. I can't let that happen."

Chou Lan said, "It's madness for you to go back into the Fyfield Valley."

"As I just explained," Tarmy said, "My daughter and my friends could be in serious trouble if I don't."

"Blackmail is a nasty crime. The victim keeps on paying," Chou lectured. "You're a case in point. You've already been blackmailed. Now you're being blackmailed again."

The comment brought a wry smile to Tarmy's lips; as an ex-police officer, he was only too well aware that blackmailers kept turning the screw if they thought they could. Despite that knowledge, he said, "This will be the last time it will happen."

"So, you're determined to go back?" Bryn said.

"I don't want to go back," Tarmy replied. "I have to go back."

"Then I'm going with you," Bryn said, "I know that place. I know the best places to attack."

When Tarmy hesitated, Bryn said, "Anto Jaks isn't the only person held prisoner up there. There are more people."

"How many?"

Bryn shrugged, "Three or four. I only saw them occasionally. I'm sure some will have died; food was always in short supply. You can't leave any survivors behind. If you do, the Great Ones will have them fed to the wolf larvae as a reprisal."

The comment made Tarmy shiver inside because he'd come to realise the Great Ones did still use that form of capital punishment. Glancing back at the air-car, Tarmy began working out if it could accommodate ten people. Did he need to take a second air-car? Satisfied he didn't, he nodded at Bryn. "Okay."

When Bryn visibly paled, Tarmy said, "Are you sure you're up to it?"

"Of course, I am," the other man replied, "I'll help you."

Bryn half-turned ready to walk toward the air-car, but Chou checked him by giving him a swift hug. While she had hold of him, she whispered, "I'm proud of you, but you need your head examined for taking the risk."

Glancing at Tarmy, she said, "I studied the hat you gave me and realised how it works." She looked at Bryn Rosslyn. "I have made some more."

Running off, she opened the boot of the second air-car and ran back. After giving Bryn a hat, she glanced at Wren and Philips.

Tarmy said, "I've given them hats, but if you've made a few more, spares could be useful to give to the people we're hopefully going to rescue."

When Chou returned with new hats, Tarmy thought about Ed Pushley. Because he was so dangerous, they'd placed a heavily shielded helmet over his head to prevent him from using his mental powers. If he ever managed to remove it, they would all be in real trouble.

Sensing his unspoken thoughts, Chou said, "Is there something the matter?"

Not wishing to worry her, Tarmy shook his head. Besides, Alton Mygael had Ed Pushley locked up in an old prison cell. It was unlikely Pushley's malign obsessions would cause him any more problems as long as Mygael made sure he didn't escape.

"Are you sure there's nothing the matter?"

"There's nothing the matter," Tarmy replied and then nodded towards Bryn Rosslyn, "It's time to go."

Both men walked away and climbed into the air-car. Wren immediately bent Tarmy's ear, "What's this guy here for?"

"He knows the Fyfield Plantation and the processing plant like the back of his hand," Tarmy replied."

When Wren looked dubious, Tarmy added, "If we're going to put the processing plant out of action, we want to cause as much damage as possible. We need to make sure the Great Ones can't carry out a few swift repairs and get it going again."

He told Alex to lead them back to the Fyfield Plantation.

As they moved off, Tarmy handed Bryn a sketching tablet and told him to draw an approximate plan of the production plant. Once he'd finished, Tarmy told him to mark the location of all significant plant items and then Tarmy ran his eye over it. "How accurate is this?"

"It's a sketch," Bryn replied defensively. "But it's reasonably accurate. As I had to walk around the processing plant, growing beds and the terraces, two or three times a week, I saw a great deal."

"What about the fuser?"

"The fuser building is there," Bryn said, pointing at his sketch. "The supply pipes look like this; shaped like a crown. There are eight mini-fusers in the same building. Each one has its own feed."

Glancing at the sketch again, Tarmy nodded, "Yeah. I see what you mean. They do look like a crown."

"They are very distinctive," Bryn agreed. "Locate the crown, and you've located the fusers."

Tarmy put his notes onto the sketch and then sent the information to Alex.

Half an hour later, the Altos and Razorback mountain ranges loomed in the distance. Eventually, the Great Rock Desert began giving way to scrub grass and clumps of multi-trunked Arcadian cacti. It was apparent they were surviving on the annual snow-melt coming off the mountains.

Once they'd crested the Altos Mountains, Alex dropped down and began weaving his way through the tops of the forest giants growing in the valleys below. Within a matter of seconds, visibility markedly decreased because fog banks began forming all around them.

Another ten kilometres in Alex joined one of the tributaries of the Fyfield River. An alert appeared on the dashboard display; the four A10s moved in close to form a box around Tarmy's air-car.

Wren shot a worried glance at Tarmy. "What's happening?"

Before Tarmy could answer, there were three explosions as

Alex took out incoming hand-launched missiles.

"What's happening?"

Tarmy shrugged, "You didn't think the Great Ones would just roll over and let us attack their plantation without a fight, did you?"

"They must have known we were going to attack them," Wren said.

"Of course, they did," Tarmy replied. "They can read our minds."

He answered Wren's unspoken question. "Even with hats on, we can't prevent some stray thoughts from reaching them. My guess is they have teams of mental listeners checking out major players. For all we know, they could have been checking out Alton Mygael."

Wren said, "I didn't expect them to have missiles."

"They've made enough money from drugs sales," Tarmy reasoned. "They can afford to buy military hardware through the black market. They don't mind paying over the odds if it gets them what they want."

His comment was confirmed by two more explosions. A few seconds later, two of the A10s peeled away and began blasting the surrounding forests with stun fire. Two Longjaws fell out of a high-level launching platform suspended across a small gorge and landed face down in the water.

With Alex urging them on, the A10s kept up the bombardment; Arcadian millipedes began dropping out of the trees in their hundreds. But instead of pulling back to avoid the stun-fire, more millipedes took their places. They began squirming out onto overhanging branches and firing venom at the passing air-car.

Inevitably some of the poison splattered onto the air-car's windshield. Reacting to the danger, Tarmy said, "When we arrive at the plantation, no one opens any doors unless I say so. And whatever you do, don't touch that stuff. It's lethal. If it gets on your skin, it will kill you in seconds. Even if it's only a small amount it will kill you. The best you can hope for is a slow lingering death."

Eventually, the air-car burst out of the side valley and began flying over the fog-shrouded Fyfield River.

Lacking Alex's radar, the A10s moved away from the banks and grouped around the air-car again. Despite the fog, from time to time, Tarmy caught a glimpse of some of the landmarks he'd passed when they'd made their escape from the Fyfield Valley; they didn't bring back good memories.

Ten minutes later, the dash screen lit up as Alex warned them the processing plant was less than five kilometres away.

The dash screen began flashing out a warning that enemy air-cars were closing in on them. A moment later, pulse fire started flashing past, and an enemy air-car shot out of the mist. One of the A10s immediately returned fire, knocking out the machine's computer and paralysing the enemy pilot.

The air-car plunged into the river and disappeared. Undeterred, two more enemy air-cars came at them out of the fog, and a lucky pulse shot punched a hole in the windscreen of Tarmy's vehicle. Fearing some of the venom splashes might get in, Tarmy opened the dash drawer and began searching for something to plug the hole. Finding a can of plastimetal foam filler, he placed it against the hole and depressed the nozzle. Although most of the foam was immediately blown away by the slipstream, some of it stuck. The pulse damage was plugged after another five-second burst.

He'd barely finished before another enemy air-car came at them, but this time two of the A10s opened fire in unison; the machine spiralled away into the river.

The processing plant loomed. Alex set about strafing the plastimetal cladding to expose the processing plant inside; he then began blasting at the individual elements in the factory. Within seconds, the whole area surrounding the plant began swarming with millipedes and armed Longjaws.

More pulse shots flashed past the air-car, the A10s moved in and mowed the opposition down like a scythe through grass. Alex went for the primary target, the fusers that powered the plant.

A few blasts later, all the processing plant's lights went out. Still, the whole area was visible because several storage tanks were on fire and flames were leaping skywards.

With the fusers destroyed, Alex set about blasting away at the terraced walls of the paddy fields closest to the processing plant. Water began cascading down, sweeping away millipedes and flooding the ground floor areas of the plant.

With the opposition mostly subdued, Tarmy turned the air-car's headlights to full beam and took it down to land following Bryn Rosslyn's instructions. A running figure cut through the headlight beams, but instead of stopping, the fleeing man began dodging and diving. The lights picked out other fleeing men.

Realising the running men were in a total panic, Tarmy called in an A10. The machine immediately bracketed the area with stun fire and brought the escapees down.

Bryn let out a howl of horror, but Tarmy cut him off. "They've only been stunned. We haven't time to chase them, even though we have droids to protect us, we can't hang around here for too long."

He pointed to the plugged-up hole in the windscreen, "We're not pushing our luck."

As if to confirm his fears, more pulse fire began flashing through the air as the Great Ones' forces recovered from the initial assault and began fighting back. Swinging the air-car around to shield the downed men, Tarmy shouted, "Come on, let's get them into the air-car but be careful of the poison."

Wren and Philips climbed out and began dragging the bodies back to the air-car; unceremoniously throwing them in. They then dived back in and slammed the doors.

They'd barely closed the doors before there was a heavy thump on the side of the air-car. The first thump was swiftly followed by more. Glancing out, Tarmy watched more and more giant Arcadian millipedes arrive and hurl themselves onto the air-car.

As Tarmy had experienced a similar event in the past, he

knew what was happening. The millipedes were weighing down the air-car, hoping to prevent its escape. Pulling out his stun gun, Tarmy began firing it at the millipedes, but it had little effect.

Re-programming the stun-gun from minimum to maximum, Tarmy fired again. However, it still appeared to have little impact on the squirming masses. Noting the colouration on the millipedes, Tarmy let out a tut of frustration as he realised why his gun didn't seem to be shifting the huge multilegged monsters. They were king millipedes, and he knew from experience they were far more robust than their smaller cousins; normal stun-fire had little effect on them.

Tarmy instructed the air-car to take off in a last-ditch attempt to dislodge them. The vehicle began shaking as it struggled with the combined weight of its human cargo and the mass of king millipedes clinging to the air-car.

Tarmy fired again and instructed the air-car to swing from side to side. As he did so, some of the millipedes that had been clinging to it began dropping off.

With the side windows cleared, Tarmy caught a glimpse of an A10 using its more powerful stun arrays to pick off more millipedes. The air-car's engines gained strength with each millipede that dropped off.

Sensing he was winning the battle, Tarmy instructed the air-car to rock from side to side again, and as more wriggling bodies fell off it surged ahead. As the machine continued to increase speed and height, Wren shouted out, "Have we picked up Anto Jaks?"

In response, Bryn Rosslyn shone a torch on the four men's faces. "This is Anto Jaks."

"Who are the other three?"

"These are the Calvert brothers," Bryn replied. "This is Brian, and this is Keith."

Bryn then answered Tarmy's unspoken question, "They're both sound."

Tarmy pointed to the fourth man, "Who's he?"

This time Bryn shook his head, "I don't know."

"No matter," Tarmy replied. "We'll find out when he recovers." He instructed the air-car to set off back to the tower by a different route. Noting the instructions, Wren queried them.

"A wise man never overflies where he's already been," Tarmy replied. "Someone on the ground might not have a chance to fire at you the first time, but he'll make sure he shoots at you if you re-trace your flight path. Make no mistake there are shed-loads of spettri down there wanting to claim our scalps."

The words had barely left Tarmy's lips before he felt something cold jar his temple. The man behind the gun gave Tarmy a yellow-toothed smile. "Cancel the last order you gave the air-car and tell it to turn around."

Tarmy realised that Yellow Tooth was the fourth man, the one that Bryn Rosslyn couldn't identify. Knowing that going back would be a death sentence, Tarmy said, "If you kill me, it will be a quicker death than being fed to the wolf larvae."

Yellow Tooth pulled the gun off Tarmy and placed it against Bryn's head. "Turn back, or I'll kill him, and then I'll shoot everyone in the air-car."

When Tarmy hesitated, Yellow Tooth pistol-whipped Bryn with the gun and screamed, "Turn back now!"

As Tarmy did as instructed, Wren gave him a worried look. In answer to the unspoken question, Tarmy said, "It looks like we picked up a spettro by mistake. Spettri are more resistant to stun fire than humans, that's why he's recovered so quickly. No doubt he was living with the captives and passing information back to the Great Ones."

Yellow Tooth smiled, but there was no humour in it, "You are very perceptive, Mr Tarleton. My masters will enjoy being reunited with you. Now instruct the air-car to descend."

Although Tarmy gave the instruction, the air-car didn't move. All they all heard was a slight bump from underneath, and then the air-car began to rise. Although he didn't comment, Tarmy guessed Alex had seen what was happening and had ordered one of the A10s to fly underneath the air-car and stop it descending. A few seconds later the air-car returned to its original course.

"What's going on?" Yellow Tooth demanded. "I'll kill this man if this vehicle doesn't turn around and descend."

Guessing that Alex had taken control of the air-car, Tarmy glanced at Yellow Tooth and said, "Sorry. I can't make it respond."

A look of real fear crossed Bryn face. But just before Yellow Tooth could fire, one of the A10s moved in close and fired a stun shot through one of the windows at point-blank range. A fraction of a second later, the passenger door next to Yellow Tooth opened and one of the A10's mechanical arms pulled the spettro out. The A10 then went into a steep dive before dumping Yellow Tooth on the ground.

The door sprang back into place, and the air-car increased speed and moved away on a new course.

Letting out a sigh of relief, Tarmy glanced back and was pleased to note that the production plant was still blazing. Wren also glanced back and started recording the damage on his percom. Noting Tarmy watching, Wren said, "Walter Verex is the sort of guy who will demand proof that we've damaged the plant."

"We've done more than damaged it. It will be out of action for months, maybe permanently." Tarmy replied. "Okay, now we've done our bit; I hope Alton Mygael is going to honour his pledges."

"He will," Wren promised and tapped 'send' on his percom. "Once Walter Verex sees these images, he'll know we've done the job, and Alton Mygael will send your people out to the tower as promised."

"Alton Mygael better had. He'll also need to keep Ed Pushley locked up. If he escapes, he'll cause no end of trouble."

"Don't worry, Alton Mygael will send your people out to the tower," Wren promised. "I'll also make sure he keeps Pushley locked up in our cells until we can work out what to do with him."

Glancing out at the Altos and Razorback mountains on the horizon, Wren added, "So where will you go now?"

Tarmy shot Bryn a warning glance before saying, "Somewhere where we can't be found. What about you? Do you *really* believe that Alton Mygael can oust Samantha and regain control?"

Wren shrugged. "Only time will tell." He felt in his pocket for the teleport boomerang device that Mih Valanson had given him and repeated, "Only time will tell."

As the air-car continued to close with the Altos Mountains, rain began hammering at the vehicle, and it began to rock alarmingly in the high winds driving the rain. Tarmy was forced to take manual control of the air-car and turn the windscreen wipers onto full power. As the heavy downpour continued, Tarmy was pleased to note the black millipede venom washing away.

After pummelling them for nearly forty minutes, the rain stopped and turned into sleet as the air-car finally crested the mountains.

Finally, after two hours, the survivor tower came back into sight, Tarmy sent one of the A10s ahead to ensure no surprises were lurking.

Once at the tower, the A10 sent back images that dispelled most of Tarmy's fears. Claire, Nonie, Red Moxstroma and the others were clearly on view, and Alton and Klaien Mygael were standing in the background.

After instructing Alex and the four A10s to deploy around the tower, Tarmy took the air-car in and landed. Claire and Nonie moved in and threw their arms around him. Although they both seemed pleased to see him, Nonie said, "Don't ever do that again."

"Do what?"

"Just fly off without telling us where you are going," she scolded.

Wren cut in. "He didn't have a lot of choice in the matter; we forced him to go back to the Fyfield Valley."

Claire and Nonie glared at him. Claire said, "How dare you!"

Wren just shrugged, "It had to be done. Sorry."

Ignoring the following stream of invective coming from both women, Wren pointed to the three stunned escapees in the back of the air-car. "Anto Jaks is coming with us; what about the other two?"

"Brian and Keith Calvert are coming with us," Bryn replied.

Once Wren and Philips had transferred Jaks to Mygael's air-car, Tarmy asked him, "Have you heard from Walter Verex?"

The other man nodded and then created a power bubble with a recorded hyperlink inside it. Amanda Tarmy's image appeared inside it with Ord Morley, Vlad Pen and Ben Lieges clustered around her. "They are granting us asylum, Dad."

Once the sequence had finished, Tarmy let out a sigh of relief, and extended his hand to Alton Mygael, "Thank you."

"You took all the risks," Mygael said.

Klaien Mygael moved in and gestured Tarmy to one side. Both Tarmy and Alton Mygael followed. Once they were away from the others, Klaien gave him another smile, "We are both pleased with what you have done."

While she was talking, Alton Mygael pushed a fat envelope into one of Tarmy's pockets.

"What's that?"

"A thank you from both of us," Mygael replied. "Don't refuse. I can afford it, and you will need the money. You and your people can't live on fresh air."

Tarmy thought about the money cards Alex had stored in his safe; he was tempted to hand the envelope back, but a quiet voice close by snapped, "Take it, Corporal Tarmy. You know there may be problems using the money in my safe."

As Mygael didn't appear to hear the voice, Tarmy realised that Alex had moved in close and had spoken to him via a whisper tube.

"Don't refuse his money," Alex urged.

Recovering, Tarmy shook Mygael's hand again and just said, "Thank you." He then added, "I think we better be on our way."

Glancing out and noting that twilight was beginning to fall, Mygael said, "It will be dark soon. Don't forget, Arcadia's natural day/night cycle is three times longer than a standard day/night cycle. It's no fun flying during at night. Why don't you come back with us for a few more days?"

Tarmy was tempted but decided against any further delay. The longer he stayed in Alton Mygael's circle, the more likely he'd be sucked back into the dark world of Salus System politics.

While Tarmy was still talking, Wren nodded to Bryn Rosslyn, took him to one side and said, "When you leave here, where are you going?"

Glancing over at Tarmy, Bryn frowned, "I'll ask the boss."

When he came back, Bryn said, "Mick doesn't want me to tell you. He wants a clean break. No links with the past."

"If you allow him to cut you off," Wren returned. "It could rebound on you."

"In what way?"

"If you isolate yourself," Wren replied. "If you lose all contact with friends, you could be in serious trouble if we can't tell you what's going on."

Thinking hard, Bryn gave Wren an address and two percom numbers. He said, "I hope I'm not going to regret telling you."

"You won't," Wren promised.

As Bryn walked away, Klaien Mygael pulled Wren to one side. Once well out of earshot, Klaien said, "As you know, Alton intends to return to Arden, but I think he's making a big mistake."

"In what way?"

"You know in what way," Klaien snapped. "Walter Verex agreed to deactivate Samantha, but I'm not sure he can."

"Why not?"

"Samantha is an Ingermann-Verex R9054 humanoid, one of the most powerful and intelligent droids ever built," Klaien replied. "She must have realised that one day someone will try to deactivate her. Don't you think she's already worked out a way of avoiding it?"

"That had occurred to me," Wren admitted. "But what can I do about it?"

"I have a plan and a favour to ask," Klaien replied.

Guessing what the favour might entail, Wren slipped his hand into his pocket and gently caressed the boomerang device Mih Valanson had made for him once more.

"Sure," Wren replied.

"Thank you," Klaien said. "Did Bryn say where they were going?"

Although Bryn had provided him with the information, Wren shook his head.

"Fraid not. Mick Tarmy told him not to. But I'm not surprised. Over the last few months, Mick Tarmy has been treated badly. He's not very trusting anymore."

Wanting to change the subject, Wren gestured towards Tarmy's group. "Shall we see them off?"

As they moved towards the two air-cars, Nonie Tomio glanced in their direction, a worried look on her face, "Have you seen Ollie?"

Klaien frowned and whispered, "Who's Ollie?"

"Her pet Arcadian pterodactyl. You must have seen it flying around," Wren whispered back, "Ollie's been a bloody nuisance. He's got a nose like a bloodhound. Once he smelt the kitchen, he was around there, knocking on the windows, scrounging food from your chefs."

"Ah! Yes, I have seen it flying around," Klaien said. "I wondered whose it was."

Nonie shouted again, "Has anyone seen Ollie?"

Wren called back, "Why don't you ask Alex to find him?"

"Good thinking," Nonie shouted and then gave instructions to Alex.

A few moments later, Ollie came flapping into view squawking loudly. As the animal kept glancing back at some unseen presence, it was apparent Alex had located Nonie Tomio's pet and had rounded him up.

With Ollie safely inside one of the air-cars, Tarmy's people climbed in; the air-cars left the tower and set off across the twilight desert with the four A10s clustered around them. Wren knew Alex was also there, guiding them on their journey towards Moxstroma's Nursery.

CHAPTER TWO

PUSHLEY FREES HIS MIND

E d Pushley heard a measured step coming from the corridor outside, and then a hatch opened. Ben Ellis called out, "Grub up, mate."

Pushley grabbed the tray without speaking and pulled it out of the guard's hands. Ellis shook his head reproachfully, "A little civility wouldn't go amiss, mate."

"Sod off," Pushley snapped back.

"Okay, be like that," Ellis replied. "Giving me a hard time won't help your case."

"Do one."

Ellis shrugged, slammed the hatch shut and then snapped the lock home.

Instead of immediately eating the food, Pushley listened to Ellis's measured footsteps receding down the corridor until he heard a distinct click as the crash bar on a fire-door operated. A slight smile formed on Pushley's lips; if his maths was correct, Ellis had just walked sixteen paces before he reached the door.

Pushley verbalised his thoughts, "Sixteen paces; if I can just get rid of this helmet, get the handcuffs off and open that door, freedom is only sixteen paces away!"

A moment later, the outer staircase door rattled and then slammed shut. As silence fell, Pushley thought about his current situation. Although his cell had two doors, as far as he was concerned, only one exit mattered. As the inner door only gave access to a small internal exercise area, it offered no means of escape.

The entrance to the corridor did though. It opened onto a hallway providing access to an escape staircase running down the back of Alton Mygael's massive house.

Once again, Pushley verbalised his thoughts, "If I can get out of here, it's straight down the fire escape, across the yard, and then I lose myself in the woods."

He then thought about Yalt, the young Ab who'd helped him so far, "If I can contact Yalt and he's still got that beat up ground-van, then ..."

Pushley's mood suddenly dropped to rock bottom, "It's all ifs ... if, if, if!"

Abandoning thoughts of escape, Pushley ran his eyes over the tray of food and let out a distinct sniff of disapproval. Having epicurean tastes, Pushley was not impressed by the meagre vegetarian main course and the bowl of mixed Arcadian fruits intended for afters. It was definitely not to his liking. Then again, being cooped up in a prison cell didn't win his approbation either.

Casting his mind back, he began thinking about his own stupidity. With so many guards patrolling the grounds, he should have realised it would end in disaster. He shouldn't have entered Alton Mygael's house. Hiding in the store cupboard alongside the conference room had also been a terrible idea.

He then thought about his abortive attempt to kill Mick Tarmy by firing through the partition wall. When he pulled the trigger instead of the stun rays going through the wall, they'd rebounded back at him.

Pushley thought about the aftermath.

While he'd still been staggering around trying to recover from the rebound blast, Mick Tarmy had pulled open the cupboard door and fired before Pushley could fire another shot.

Going through the post-mortem of his failure, Pushley recalled something that Alton Mygael had said. According to him, the partition walls had been deliberately lined with special anti-stun blast paper during the occupation to reduce the risk of possible terrorist attacks. Pushley let out another curse and then muttered, "Just my luck to come to a house with anti-stun paper on the walls.

His thoughts then returned to his bête noire, "I hate you, Tarmy!"

He then added, "It might take me a lifetime, but I'm going to get even with you, Tarmy."

He then revised his comment. Picking up an Arcadian banana from the fruit bowl with his free hand, Pushley brandished it like a gun and mouthed, "Bang, bang, bang. I'm going to get even with all three of them, Tarmy, Hyndman and Tomio."

He grinned, "I'm going to kill Tarmy and his two witches. But not before, I've made them suffer."

After thinking about Tarmy, Hyndman and Tomio's fate for a few minutes longer, Pushley remembered the tray he was holding and began scooping up food with his bare hands and stuffing it into his mouth. While he was still eating, his thoughts then changed to his arrest and incarceration

Although Pushley couldn't recall much after being shot by Mick Tarmy, he vaguely remembered being dragged towards the cell he was in. As Ellis was bringing him food, simple logic dictated he was still in Alton Mygael's house. If he was in a police cell, it would have been a local police officer bringing him food, not Ellis.

Pushley began studying his surroundings. The only thing that didn't make sense was the cell itself. As it was stoutly built from reinforced plastimetal, there appeared to be a contradiction; how many residential houses had purpose-made prison cells?

Once he'd finished the vegetarian first course, Pushley threw the empty bowl at an undomed observation camera in one corner of the room. When there was a dull clunk, and the lens obligingly swung to one side, Pushley laughed, "I wonder if I can do it again."

After taking a few bites out of the fruit, he then hurled the second bowl at the camera, and it obligingly swung to face a blank wall. In the hope that Ellis might still be close by despite the outer door slamming shut, Pushley shouted out, "I'm going to get out of here, Ellis. Mark my words."

Getting no response, Pushley sighed. Then, bit by bit, his anger began to rise again. Anger turned to frustration, and he started slamming the heavy isolation helmet they'd forced onto his head against the cell wall. After headbanging for nearly five minutes, he was on the point of giving up from exhaustion when there was a distinct cracking sound, and he realised he'd managed to damage the accursed helmet.

Turning to face a small mirror hanging on one wall, Pushley tried to ascertain how much damage he'd caused but swiftly realised there was nothing visible. Cursing under his breath again, he slumped back on his bed, but just before he could leap back into the dark well of despair, his mind filled with vague images. As more images began coalescing, Pushley let out a whoop of delight, "I can mind-read again!"

As he began trawling the ether, searching for contacts, Pushley started thinking about Tarmy, Hyndman and Tomio again. With hate driving him on, he tried to mind-link with his three most hated foes.

After expending nearly ten minutes on his search, he finally mind-linked with Mick Tarmy but swiftly withdrew when his mind filled with a barrage of horrific images. After trying to counter the barrage, Pushley retired. Not only was mind-linking with Tarmy pointless, it was sapping his strength.

He attempted to mind-link with Claire Hyndman. As he was totally rebuffed, he concluded that a monarch's mind must have a different configuration than a normal human brain. Claire Hyndman's mind was sealed to him; it was like running into a brick wall.

Giving up on Hyndman, Pushley tried to mind-link with Nonie Tomio but suddenly found another subject entirely.

He caught a glimpse of Nonie Tomio and realised how he was seeing her. Nonie had a pet Arcadian pterodactyl called Ollie and Pushley was seeing Nonie through the animal's eyes.

While he watched, Nonie carefully removed her clothes and then moved towards a primitive water shower. As she stepped under the shower and began washing her lithe body, Pushley felt his lower abdomen reacting to the visual stimulation.

Without prompting, he began to reminisce; he recalled the time he'd spent at Fort Saunders. Nonie Tomio had been there too.

After staring at Nonie's naked body for a while, his lust turned to anger. For a second or two, the strength of his emotions surprised him. He then had an epiphany; he was not a man who liked to take no for an answer. One of the reasons he hated Nonie so much was because she'd always spurned his advances. While based at Fort Saunders, he'd had several short-term relationships with several women. Nonie hadn't been one of them.

The second reason for hating her was jealousy; she'd now chosen to live with Mick Tarmy, his bête noire.

Pulling his eyes away from Nonie, Pushley instructed Ollie to look around the shower room. As the walls were nothing more than badly painted blockwork, Pushley's mind began to whir. The poor quality of the finish hinted at the back o' beyond.

Losing interest in Nonie, Pushley instructed Ollie to go outside and fly around. Once the pterodactyl was airborne, Pushley took in the surroundings. Although it was night, Ollie's infrared vision gave Pushley a clear view.

Other than a few white flat roof houses clustered around a small palm-fringed lake, the only other building of any note was an eight-bedroom motel, a general store and an air-car charging station. Within seconds, he realised they looked familiar. As he'd stayed at Nabid Oasis several times while he'd been traversing the Great Rock Desert, he realised where Nonie was.

As Ollie continued to fly around the small oasis, Pushley saw two air-cars parked in charging bays and guessed that they belonged to Mick Tarmy. The only unanswered question was why Nonie Tomio and Mick Tarmy were at Nabid Oasis.

After Ollie has been flying around for some time, Pushley detected mental resistance and realised that the pterodactyl had sensed his presence. A moment later, Pushley lost contact with the flying reptile.

Annoyed by the sudden turn of events, Pushley began searching for a link with Nonie. Within seconds, he linked and vaguely enjoyed the sensation of water flowing down her naked body.

Encouraged by her willing acceptance, Pushley began probing, asking her to explain why she was at Nabid. He obtained the answer with little difficulty. Nonie's mind said, "Mick is taking us to start a new life in New Victoria."

Pushley immediately latched onto the pro-noun and demanded, "Who's us?"

"Claire and I," Nonie's mind answered.

"So, you and Claire are still with Tarmy?"

"Yes, we're partners."

More out of spite than a necessity, Pushley mind thought, "You do realise that Claire is a monarch."

"Yes."

"Doesn't that revolt you?"

"Why should it?"

Pushley shuddered. As he'd worked with monarchs during the last system war, he'd swiftly grown to loathe them. They weren't natural.

"She's been genetically modified," Pushley mind spoke.

So?"

"Doesn't that worry you?"

"No. I love Claire."

Although surprised by the response, Pushley didn't pursue the possible implications of the last comment. Instead, he said, "What about Mick Tarmy. Do you love Mick?"

"Of course," Nonie's mind replied. "And he loves Claire and me."

"Does Mick Tarmy know that Claire's a monarch?"

"Yes."

"Doesn't that revolt or worry him either?"

"No."

Pushley was tempted to continue with the same line of interrogation but decided not to bother. Nonie's answers made it clear that Tarmy's ménage à trois was still intact.

Once again, the knowledge annoyed Pushley intensely.

As the internal anger grew, Pushley abandoned subtlety and demanded, "Where is my bag with the money cards in it?"

Nonie responded to the mental interrogation by allowing Pushley access to her recent memories. A moment later Pushley found himself in a huddle with Tarmy, Nonie and Claire. There was an object that looked like a small, oddly shaped bedframe, lying on a table. After interrogating Nonie's mind, he realised the bedframe was Alex, their TK5 but the droid had dropped its invisibility cloak.

While he was still reading Nonie's memories, Mick Tarmy said, "What I'm about to show you must go no further. Understood?"

When both women nodded, Tarmy told Alex to open his safe and then pulled out a highly ornamented bag.

Pushley reacted immediately, "My bag. I thought so! They have got my bag!"

After unlocking the bag, Tarmy tipped out the contents.

Claire's jaw dropped, and she let out a slight whistle, "How much is there?"

"Thirty million Enron Dollars," Tarmy replied. "Roughly equivalent to Ten million ACU."

"But where did this come from?" Nonie said.

Tarmy glanced at the droid, "Maybe you can explain better Alex."

Alex was brief, "I found the bag and informed Corporal Tarmy it was spoils of war."

The comment sparked jealousy and Claire shot Tarmy a blinding look, "Alex is my droid, and you've taken him off me."

"No, I haven't," Tarmy replied. "Alex has accepted me as the leader of this group because of my old army and police rank. Military droids do that automatically. Once they've locked onto a leader, they follow that person. It's part of their programming. They take orders from the person they perceive to be their controller or the person holding the most senior rank."

"Which is why Alex has taken to calling you Corporal Tarmy," Claire observed.

"Correct."

Being in a liverish mood, Claire became personal, "Corporal is not a very high rank, is it? Less than a sergeant."

Sensing she was just lashing out, Tarmy ignored the slight, "As you say, a corporal is lower than a sergeant."

"But as far as Alex is concerned, you out-rank me?"

"As I said, it's a programming issue," Tarmy replied. "Admittedly, a corporal is not very high in the military pecking order, but Alex still accepts me as being the person in the group holding the highest rank."

Instead of answering, Claire went very quiet. Suddenly, her face started to alter its shape, and her hair began changing from blonde to copper. Knowing what was about the happen, Tarmy snapped, "No! Please, don't start that! I don't like it when you start to metamorphose in front of me. It's creepy."

"It's happening because you're making me nervous, Mick," Claire replied.

"Well there's no need to be nervous," Tarmy assured her.

"I have every reason to be nervous," Claire replied. "You've taken control of Alex and…"

Sensing they were headed for trouble, Tarmy cut in, "Look. Let's not go into the whys and wherefores now. We can discuss this later. Besides, we shouldn't get ahead of ourselves. Legally this money should be handed in."

Claire said, "Handed in!"

"If we keep it, legally it could be deemed stealing by finding," Tarmy replied.

Nonie said, "There would be a reward, though."

The words had barely left her mouth before Alex extended a mechanical arm, grabbed the bag, dragged it back into his safe, and the door crashed shut, "The money stays with me."

Claire said, "What's going on?"

As Tarmy had been expecting Alex to react in the way he had, he didn't bat an eyelid. Instead, he said, "Alex has already proclaimed the bag to be spoils of war, his programming has cut in, and he's unlikely to allow the bag to be handed in."

Nonie frowned, "Is Alex allowed to do that?"

"Alex was for the most part, responsible for defeating Irrelevant at the river island battle," Tarmy explained. "It was a battle, and as far as he is concerned, the Singburn Convention applies. He's allowed to claim the money as spoils of war for his group."

Claire eyed Tarmy thoughtfully. She said, "You knew he'd do this, didn't you?"

Tarmy shook his head, "I suspected he might, but I didn't know."

Nonie sounded an upbeat note, "Well, that's the problem solved then. We keep the money."

"No, it's not a problem solved, "Tarmy said. "If we keep the money, there could still be a sting in the tail."

Nonie said, "And what sting is that?"

Calling upon his police experience, Tarmy said, "Most of the criminal world like using Eron Dollars because Eron is a tax haven. Eron banks won't supply information on their clients to external tax authorities."

"Where is this leading?" Claire said.

"Unfortunately, if we present some of the larger denomination money cards to a bank on Arcadia, questions will be asked."

"What sort of questions?" Nonie said.

"Even on Arcadia, the authorities try to prevent criminals from money laundering," Tarmy replied. "If we present a very high denomination money card, we are likely to be asked where it came from."

"So, the cards will be of no use to us."

"I didn't say that," Tarmy replied. "Some of them are low denomination, and it may be possible to drain the funds and transfer them to other cards to prevent challenges. The only problem is I don't know how to do that."

"So, we can use the money if we are careful…?"

Before Tarmy could answer, Pushley felt his mental powers reaching exhaustion, and his grip on Tomio began to fade. As the psychic link broke, Pushley let out a wail of despair, "They've got my money!"

CHAPTER THREE

AWIS OASIS: YALT AGREES TO HELP PUSHLEY ESCAPE

Yalt caught a glimpse of Connell and instinctively knew that the other man was looking for him. His fears were confirmed when Connell began running in his direction. Yalt didn't think; he began to run as fast as his legs would carry him.

Leaving the main square, he darted down a side alley and began dodging and weaving down even narrower alleyways. Glancing over his shoulder, Yalt caught a glimpse of Connell and realised that despite his speed and evasive tactics he hadn't thrown off his pursuer. He was about to race towards another side-turning when he stumbled.

Catching a glimpse of Hal Warmers as he went down, Yalt realised the other man had been lying in wait and had tripped him. He cursed; he'd fallen into a carefully laid trap. Like lions working as a team, Connell had driven him into a killing zone, and Hal Warmers had pounced. As he attempted to regain his feet, Yalt also realised that Warmers had chosen a good place for an ambush. Not only was the narrow alley deserted it also lacked street cameras, and Connell was close by to assist if he fought back.

Hal Warmers moved in fast, dragged Yalt to his feet and then pinned him against a wall, "Right! As you've been ignoring my calls, I thought it was time we had another very personal chat."

Knowing what Warmers was going to ask, Yalt bleated, "I have not seen Mr Pushley, padrone. Honest!"

"So, he's not contacted you?"

"No padrone."

Being in a disbelieving mood, Warmers grabbed hold of Yalt's little finger and twisted it. He then repeated, "Have you seen Ed Pushley?"

"No, padrone," Yalt bleated. "The last time I saw Mr Pushley was when I dropped him off at the big house."

Warmers said, "Alton Mygael's house at the top of Central Lake? The one we were looking at when the alarms went off."

"Yes, padrone. That house."

In the hope of avoiding more punishment, Yalt went into grovel mode; "I said I would tell you if I saw him again, but I haven't seen him." He then added, "I think Mr Mygael is holding Mr Pushley prisoner."

After twisting Yalt's little finger again, Warmers said, "What makes you say that?"

Instead of answering Yalt let out a squeal of pain, "You're hurting me."

After easing the pressure on Yalt's finger slightly, Warmers said, "Then tell me what I want to know."

"Tolan, my brother, knows someone who works at Mr Mygael's house," Yalt said. "He's been told they have Mr Pushley locked up."

Warmers frowned, "Locked up! Locked up where?"

"They are keeping him prisoner, in a cell."

Warmers' frown increased; ordinary houses didn't have cells, "Keeping him prisoner in a cell? That's illegal! False imprisonment! Anyway, how come they've got cells at Alton Mygael's house?"

Realising Warmers didn't believe him, Yalt added, "They do have cells in Mr Mygael's house, padrone. They are not allowed to remove them. They are features of local interest. They were put in during the occupation. The Ardenese military once occupied Mr Mygael's house."

Sensing the other man was probably telling the truth, Warmers released Yalt's finger from his vice-like grip. In Awis Oasis, most of the houses had had restrictions placed upon them to preserve the past. If the Ardenese military had built cells, the chances were they were protected and couldn't be demolished or dismantled. With tourism forming a significant part of the Awis Oasis economy, retaining features of local interest had become a regional obsession. Wealthy, rubbernecking tourists liked staring at native oddities and taking pictures of themselves in front of them.

Warmers said, "Why have they got him locked up?"

"He tried to kill Mr Mygael and several other people," Yalt replied.

Warmer's eyebrows rose slightly, "He did what?"

"He tried to shoot several people at Mr Mygael's house," Yalt repeated.

"So why haven't they handed him over to the police?" Warmer's demanded. "Attempted murder is a serious offence."

"They don't want to hand him over to the police. Tolan says Mr Mygael thinks Mr Pushley is a spettro and the police wouldn't know what to do with him."

Fear and respect entered Yalt's voice. "Tolan says Mr Mygael thinks it would be dangerous to hand Mr Pushley over to the police because he can invade people's minds."

"Look," Warmers said, "I thought Pushley had invaded my mind when we met up in my bar a short time ago. But I swiftly came to the conclusion he hadn't. I think he drugged my drink. I've met a few spettri over the years when I've done deals for the Great Ones. In my experience, spettri rely on their mental skills to enforce their will. Pushley shot me with a stun gun. It's not the actions of a spettro. In any case, spettri can't leave the Fyfield Valley or the Altos Plateaux. If they leave, they die very soon afterwards."

"I think Mr Pushley is a special spettro," Yalt said, "Special spettri can leave the Fyfield Valley."

Warmers' face showed contempt, "I hope you don't expect me to believe the horseshit you're spouting;" he released his grip and stepped back. "Just so we don't misunderstand one another, Ed Pushley owes me a lot of money Yalt, and I intend to get it back off him. If he contacts you, I want to know immediately, understood?"

When Yalt nodded, Warmers walked away.

Fearing Hal Warmers might change his mind and renew his attack, Yalt took to his heels. After covering the best part of two hundred metres, he slowed down, panting hard. It was only then he realised he'd left his hat behind, the one he'd carefully stitched with special beads to ward off mind invaders. Glancing back, he was tempted to return to where he'd been ambushed but changed his mind. It wasn't worth the risk of running into Warmers and Connell again, and hats were cheap; he could always make another.

He began walking to a semi-derelict building that provided basic shelter for several people like him.

Once inside, he made his way up to one of the upper floor rooms. Nearing the top, he broke out into a sweat because the flat roof was lacking in insulation. His older brother, Tolan, eyed him thoughtfully as he walked in, "Have you been in a fight?"

As there was no point in lying, Yalt nodded, "Yeah."

Family loyalties cut in, and Tolan bristled; he was a man willing to take up the cudgels on behalf of his younger sibling, "Who with?"

Yalt was tempted to name names but resisted. Although Tolan was bigger and more powerfully built than he was, taking on the likes of Hal Warmers and his hired thugs was only asking for trouble. Tolan might end up severely injured or worse, dead.

When he didn't reply, Tolan said, "So, who's been picking on you?"

Yalt dodged the question, "I said leave it! It doesn't matter. I can deal with it myself. I'd better get cleaned up."

Pulling aside a curtain, he stepped into an alcove that served as the toilet and wash area. Once he'd drawn the curtain behind him, Yalt glanced at his face in the cloudy, black-spotted mirror hanging on the wall. Seeing bleeding lacerations, Yalt guessed he'd scraped his face against the wall when Warmers had tripped him up.

Yalt began cranking an old hand pump and partially filled the basin with discoloured tank water. Once he'd washed away most of the blood, he glanced in the mirror again.

He was about to continue when his vague reflection disappeared, and a strange luminescent greenness replaced it. Yalt thought about the Arcadian myths, that his people, the Ab, believed. Stories about the survivors that escaped from The Wreck, the burnt out starship that still orbited Arcadia. He thought about the myths concerning the Great Ones, and the green caves where the Great Ones were supposed to live, and he wasn't surprised when a spettro dressed in clerical garb suddenly appeared in the mirror.

Smiling, the high priest spoke to him, but his words come from inside Yalt's mind, "Do you know who I am?"

Although Yalt didn't know precisely who the cleric was, the ancient Arcadian myths supplied the answer. The high ranking spettro worked for the Great Ones, the masters of the Fyfield Valley and Altos Plateaux.

"Well? Do you know who I am?"

Yalt nodded and thought spoke, "Yes, your eminence."

"Good," the high priest said. "That saves me having to explain - Now then, I believe you've been working for Ed Pushley."

When Yalt nodded again, the cleric said, "Where is he?"

When Yalt didn't answer, something entered his skull, and a fat slug began slip-sliding over his brain, searching for facts. Yalt cursed; if he hadn't lost his beaded hat during his fight with Hal Warmers, the high priest wouldn't have been able to probe his mind so quickly and so profoundly.

After a few seconds had elapsed, the cleric mind spoke to him again, "So Ed Pushley's being imprisoned by our enemy, Alton Mygael."

"I didn't know Alton Mygael was your enemy, your eminence," Yalt mind replied. "But yes, Ed Pushley is being imprisoned by Alton Mygael."

"You believe Ed Pushley is a spettro, don't you?"

"Yes," Yalt said, "But I also know that it is unlikely. Everyone knows, if a spettro leaves the Fyfield Valley or the Altos Plateaux, Death swiftly follows them."

"Not everyone knows that," the cleric corrected. "Many outworlders know very little about the Great Ones and our followers. However, you are correct; there is an unknown force that traps our people in the Fyfield Valley and the Altos Plateaux."

Yalt mind spoke again, "Then how could Ed Pushley be a spettro?"

"I believe there is a reason for that," the cleric explained. The image in the cloudy mirror suddenly changed and began displaying an event sequence of three Arcadian plesiosaurs attacking a low flying air-car. As the attack continued, the high priest mind spoke again, "Observe this. The person who is about to die is a spettro."

A moment later, one of the Arcadian plesiosaurs put its head through the air-car's open roof door, grabbed one of the men inside by his upper torso, pulled him out of the air-car and dragged him underwater.

The high priest said, "There is your answer."

When Yalt's mind didn't react, the cleric explained; "The spettro who died transferred his essence into Ed Pushley just before the plesiosaur killed him."

"Essence?"

"You would probably call it a spirit or soul," the high priest replied.

Not being of a religious persuasion, Yalt found it hard to believe anyone had a soul; death was death, nothing survived.

The cleric picked up on his misgivings, "Whether you believe that spettri have an essence, what you call a soul, is of no importance to me; I believe there has been a transfer."

He then added, "If Ed Pushley possesses the powers of a spet-tro, then he could be very useful to us."

Yalt frowned, "In what way?"

"If he agrees to work with us, he could help us do what we've been trying to do for years," The cleric said.

"And what's that?"

"Help the Great Ones to escape from this wretched planet that your people call Arcadia. Ed Pushley could also help us take revenge on our enemies."

Yalt thought, "What do you want from me?"

"I've told you; your help."

"With what?"

"Ed Pushley is being held against his will by our enemies."

"By enemies do you mean Alton Mygael?

"We have many enemies," the high priest mind spoke. "At the moment the main ones are Walter Verex, Mick Tarleton, also known as Mick Tarmy, Alton Mygael and Allus Wren. As Ed Pushley is at Alton Mygael's house, you are in a position to be of assistance to us."

Yalt's frown increased, "I still do not know what you want from me."

"Despite the mind shield he has been forced to wear; we sense that Ed Pushley is trying to escape. If he does escape and asks for your help, I want you to do as he asks."

When Yalt didn't respond, the cleric added, "I will make sure that Ed Pushley rewards you if you help him."

When Yalt remained silent, the cleric began delving into Yalt's mind again and realised why he was mentally prevaricat-ing. Many years before, during one of the Great Ones' pogroms against the Ab population, Yalt's family had fled from the Fy-field Valley in terror and crossed the desert to reach Awis Oasis. Many of them had died on the way. As Yalt considered the Great Ones to be his enemy, he didn't want to co-operate.

Plunging deep in Yalt's mind, the high priest did his best to temporarily alter Yalt's perceptions on life. Once he'd managed to temporarily suppress Yalt's historical memories, the cleric repeated, "Will you help Ed Pushley?"

This time Yalt nodded and thought, "Yes, your eminence."

"Good!" the high priest responded. "A caution: If you tell Hal Warmers about our discussions, I will punish you. Understood?"

When Yalt nodded, the images in the mirror disappeared, and Yalt let out a massive sigh of relief. Although he had agreed to co-operate with the high priest, he still feared him. The sudden expulsion of breath made Tolan call out, "Are you all right in there, bruv?"

Yalt called back, "Yeah. I'm fine," and then emerged from behind the curtain.

Tolan glanced at the scratches and bruising on Yalt's face again, but instead of attempting to find out who'd beaten him up, he said, "Will you be well enough to go to work?"

Yalt nodded, "I'm okay, really."

It was a half-truth, and they both knew it. As only Tolan and he had jobs, taking time off work wasn't an option. Besides, working at the teleport centre was hardly arduous work; it was just programming the teleport; pushing buttons. Yalt was also in a position to beg for the stale food. Coming home with bags of curled up sandwiches, vegetarian sausage rolls, unused cartons of Kimchi and tubs of out of date coleslaw helped prevent Yalt's extended family from starving.

"That's good," Tolan said, "When are you going to take Ullin's van back?"

Thinking about what the high priest had just told him, that Ed Pushley might need rescuing Yalt said, "I might need it again, so I'll hang onto it."

"Don't keep it too long," Tolan cautioned. "If you do, Ullin might not lend it to us again."

"I won't keep it too long," Yalt promised.

CHAPTER FOUR
ARRIVAL AT MOXTROMA'S NURSERY

As the air-car got closer to the nursery, Red Moxstroma's face showed on Tarmy's air-car dash, and his voice came over the intercom from the other air-car. "We can't be far now. We should be able to see the nursery shortly."

With the whole area being in the grip of Arcadia's long night, Tarmy ordered the four A10s to floodlight the ground below. Red smiled and then said, "There it is. Home sweet home."

The words had barely crossed his lips before he added, "Oh! No."

"What's the matter?"

"Look!"

Everyone in the air-cars glanced out. Claire Hyndman said, "What are we supposed to be looking at, Red?"

"It's what we're not looking at," Red replied bitterly. "It's appalling."

"What is?"

This time Bryn Rosslyn's face appeared on screen and his voice chipped in, "Look at the main house. Every window's been smashed, and our mechanical plant's missing. All the growing tunnels have gone too. They've taken everything. The whole place has been stripped."

Tarmy was tempted to ask who was likely to have stripped the nursery but let the issue slide. As an ex-police officer, he'd half expected to find devastation. With Red and Bryn being held captive by the Great Ones for over two years, the local criminal element would have had more than enough time to take anything of value.

While Tarmy was still thinking, Bryn added, "Believe it or not, that was a field down by the river. Now it's completely flooded."

Red's face reappeared, "What a mess! The whole place has gone to rack and ruin. It's totally run down. It'll cost a fortune to put this place back to rights."

"I'm sure we'll manage," Tarmy replied.

"How?"

Instead of continuing the debate, Tarmy instructed the four A10s to hover over the nursery and then ordered both air-cars to land close to the farmhouse. Once they'd touched down, Tarmy, Claire and Nonie went to the other air-car. Tarmy said, "Let's have a look around. Let's have a walk and a talk."

Red Moxstroma, Bryn Rosslyn, Chou Lan and Brian and Keith Calvert joined them. Rather pointedly, Lascaux Kurgan remained where she was, obviously determined not to get her shoes dirty.

Tarmy moved toward the old farmhouse and glanced inside. As the fittings, boiler, radiators and pipework had been stripped out, the place was basically just a shell

Red spoke his mind, "It'll cost a fortune to repair this. We're finished."

"It just depends on whether you're serious about getting this place repaired or abandoning it," Tarmy observed.

"It's not just the farmhouse," Red snapped. "It's everything."

"Okay," Tarmy said. "Let me rephrase that. Are you giving up or are we going to get this place sorted out?"

Bryn said, "Have you got an idea, Mick?"

Tarmy was tempted to tell Bryn about Pushley's money but decided against it; alienating Alex would be a bad move.

"I'm sure we'll manage to get your nursery back on its feet."

"How?"

Instead of providing an answer, Tarmy replied, "Tell me what you need, and I'll try and finance it."

"How?"

Cornered, Tarmy told them about the money that Alton Mygael had given him and said, "If we back you, Claire, Nonie and myself will need to be stakeholders in the business."

"It'll take a lot of money to put this place to rights," Red grumbled.

Without prompting, Alex spoke to Tarmy using his whisper probe, "I will let you use some of Irrelevant's money to help them. Do you need me to prove you have the money to finance them?"

Echoing Alex, Tarmy said, "Do you need me to prove to you I have the money to finance you?"

"It would be helpful," Red replied, "We need assurances."

Although Tarmy was unsure what would happen next, he said, "Okay, I'll prove it."

A moment later, ten money cards appeared out of nowhere and began dancing around in mid-air. Then a power bubble formed, and the cards began reporting their worth. The power bubble calculated their total worth at two hundred thousand Eron dollars.

After floating the cards enticingly in front of Red and Bryn for a full ten seconds, the money and the bubble disappeared.

When both men just look surprised, Tarmy said, "You can do a lot of repairs for two hundred thousand Eron dollars."

Red came back with, "We might need more."

"Take it or leave it," Tarmy countered.

"We'll take it," Bryn replied. "What do we do now?"

"Go through everything with Red and make a list of what we need, and any reliable local contractors you know."

"And where are we going to make a list? Down there?" Red snapped back. "The whole place is a wreck."

"I don't think that will be necessary," Tarmy replied and instructed the A10's to take up residence in what remained of an old barn. He told Alex to follow the air-cars.

Red was suspicious, "What are you doing?"

Tarmy gestured toward the air-cars, "We obviously can't stay here."

"So, what have you got in mind?"

In response, Tarmy said, "We'll have to find a hotel."

Red's mouth dropped open, "A hotel!"

"Alton Mygael is paying," Tarmy replied. "And once we have a roof over our heads, we can make plans."

"What plans?" Bryn demanded.

"We'll ask a few local contractors to quote for renovating the house, providing us with temporary accommodation and installing a proper security fence," Tarmy said. "It may take a few weeks to get this place back on its feet. But we'll get there."

"It could take months," Red replied. "We can't stay in a hotel for months."

"We won't need to," Tarmy replied optimistically. "Once we have some temporary cabins here, we'll come back here."

Brian Calvert pointed to himself and his brother, "What about us?"

Bryn Rosslyn said, "Don't worry lads. If you want jobs, there'll be plenty to do around here."

CHAPTER FIVE

WREN INTERVIEWS PUSHLEY

Walking down the corridor, Wren couldn't help but glance back at the four grim-looking cells at the far end. He was tempted to walk towards them and peek in at Pushley but Halsworth Levan, one of the senior guards, noted his interest and shook his head, "Not a good idea Senior Group Leader."

Wren eyed him thoughtfully and then said, "I don't use my rank anymore, Halsworth."

"As you wish, sir."

Nodding towards Pushley's cell, Wren said. "Any problems?"

"No, sir."

"What about exercise?"

"His cell has two doors," Levan revealed. "One leads onto this corridor. The other gives access to an exercise room. He's allowed two hours of exercise a day. And before you ask, we don't remove his helmet except to allow him to wash. His helmet is never removed unless there are several guards in the room. Mr Mygael has explained to us all that he thinks Mr Pushley is a spettro."

"He might be," Wren agreed. "But we can't be sure at this stage."

Ignoring the comment, Levan then added, "Since Mr Pushley was placed in the cell, Mr Mygael has fully briefed all the guards concerning spettri. We know where they come from and how dangerous they are."

"It looks like you have everything covered," Wren conceded and then walked towards the conference room. Entering, he realised that Alton Mygael wasn't alone. Klaien was with him.

Alton Mygael glanced up from his desk and said, "Thank you for coming to see me, Allus. I want your opinion."

"About what?"

"What are we going to do about Ed Pushley? As you know, at the moment we've got him locked up in a cell."

"You could hand him over to the local police."

"We can't do that," Mygael said. "He's a spettro."

Mygael then added, "In the old days, when we were Zadernaster boys, we always dealt with things our way. Going to the police would have been unthinkable."

"That was a long time ago," Wren replied. "I still think you should call the police."

Mygael's jaw jutted pugnaciously as his stubborn streak cut in, "I haven't handed Pushley over to the local police because I am convinced, he is a spettro. If we hand him over, the police will just treat him like a normal criminal."

"Which to them, he is."

"But we know the truth," Mygael snapped. "He is a spettro."

"You're probably right," Wren conceded, "But we don't know for sure."

Klaien cut into the conversation, "What exactly is a spettro?"

"Mutant humanoids who work for the Great Ones," Wren replied. "They can read minds. Some really powerful spettri can also make normal people do their bidding."

Glancing at Klaien, Alton Mygael became patronising, "I'll explain in more detail later, my dear."

Annoyed, Klaien snapped, "Tell me now."

"Like Allus just said, they're mutant human beings," Mygael replied, "They were created by the Great Ones using stolen human DNA. They combined it with their DNA or whatever their bodies are made from and created a hybrid, an abomination. Spettri come in a variety of types. The Great Ones have selectively bred them for different functions."

Klaien's eyebrows shot up, "You mean they have done the same thing to us as we've done to dogs? They've bred different types of spettro to suit their purposes?"

"That's an excellent analogy," Alton Mygael agreed. He added, "So you get ugly workers, ones that look like us and there is also a four-armed variant according to Mick Tarmy. Like I said, some spettri are damn ugly; others can easily pass as humans."

Klaien said, "Why do the Great Ones make spettri?"

"The spettri locked up at Minton Isolation Facility 1 were sent to Arden to create a fifth column," Alton Mygael replied, "And just because I've been forced to leave Arden doesn't mean I've given up the fight."

"What exactly are you fighting?"

"The spettri sent to Arden were supposed to take over. If they'd succeeded in bringing Arden under their control, they were supposed to bring some of the Great Ones to Arden. Their next objective, taking over the whole of the Salus System. Luckily we found out in time and started arresting them and placing them in isolation units before they could cause any real harm."

Mygael glanced at Wren, "As we both know, the arrests were all hush-hush, of course."

"Why?" Klaien asked.

"Because under Section 32 of the Consolidated Space Agreement, we should have treated the spettri as a dangerous alien species and placed Arden into quarantine. We should also have notified the other Salus System colonies as soon as the first spettro was discovered."

"But you didn't."

"Closing down our mining operations would have cost a small fortune," Mygael replied. "Something similar happened on Tagus 5. They went through the procedure. But instead of being helped, they were shunned by the whole system. The Tagus 5 scenario convinced our board of directors that the same thing could happen on Arden if we sent in a notification. We decided to ignore Section 32, and deal with the spettri ourselves.

That is still the situation."

Mygael continued, "Anyway, we digress, let's return to what we were originally discussing. Even though we are not far from the Fyfield Valley, most of the locals are now outworlders who have settled on this planet."

"The few remaining Ab may believe in the Great Ones, but the outworlders certainly don't. To them, the Great Ones are just a myth; a fairy story; like the abominable snowman. So, it's unlikely the police will believe us if we try to explain just how dangerous Pushley is. Don't forget, Pushley tried to kill us all."

Mygael added, "If they don't believe us and Pushley is allowed to escape or roam free the chances are, he'll come after us again. We can't take the risk. Next time he might succeed in killing us. We have to deal with it ourselves."

After some thought, Wren nodded, "I've seen the spettri you had locked up at Minton Isolation Facility 1. They looked an evil bunch. We also had a run-in with a spettro during our attack on the Fyfield plantation. We dubbed him, Yellow Tooth. Yellow Tooth tried to take over the air-car. He was a fanatic, quite prepared to kill everyone in the air-car for his cause. If Pushley is a spettro, then I agree, he's highly dangerous. But he may just be insane."

"You think so," Mygael replied.

"Pushley's an archaeologist; he was born on Midway, not in the Fyfield Valley; you're claiming he's a spettro. How does that work?" Wren replied.

Mygael shrugged, "If it looks like a gorilla, grunts like a gorilla and thumps its chest like a gorilla, then the chances are it is one. As Pushley's exhibiting all the attributes of a spettro, we have to accept he is one and we can't let him escape. So, do we keep him locked up or do we kill him?"

Despite his years in the Zadernaster Boys when street killing was commonplace, Wren bridled. Since escaping from the streets, he'd put wanton killing behind him, "Whatever he is, we can't just kill him in cold blood."

Mygael shrugged, "Okay if you rule out killing him, the only option we have is to keep him under lock and key until I take over from Samantha. Then we will be able to transfer Pushley to Minton Isolation Facility 1 and lock him up with all the other spettri. That's what I think."

"It's a plan," Wren agreed. "Do you mind if I talk to Pushley?"

"By all means," Mygael said. "I'll arrange for Ben Ellis to let you into his cell. But don't take any risks. Pushley is dangerous."

Wren was about to stand up and leave, but Klaien said, "I need to say something."

Alton Mygael's tone became particularly frosty, "What about?"

"You know what about," Klaien replied. "This stupid idea of you returning to Arden."

"I have to go back," Alton Mygael said. "It's my duty."

"It's a trap," Klaien said. "I'm convinced of it. Samantha hasn't been deactivated, and she's luring you back, Alton."

In response, Alton Mygael created a hyperlink. Eventually, Walter Verex's CGI appeared in a power bubble.

Mygael said, "My apologies for contacting you again, Walter. There is some concern our end about Samantha. Are you sure she's been deactivated?"

Verex said, "You might like to see this."

Samantha's image appeared in the bubble. The display panel near to the top of her conical body then enlarged; instead of displaying her regular arrogant face, the panel was showing the word, "Retired."

A moment later, a Black-Clad officer appeared and made an urgent request for assistance. Verex's image returned and said, "I promised to deactivate Samantha; I've done it."

Mygael said, "This means we can return to Arden."

"It certainly does."

Once the power bubble image had evaporated, Mygael said, "We have now had a positive confirmation. So, I'm going back."

A slight smile then formed on his face, "In fact. I've already booked a slot at the local teleport. The three of us are going back."

"Who's the three?"

Mygael smiled at Wren. "Wren, Philips and me. Us Zadernaster boys are back together."

~*~

Ben Ellis began jingling his keys, but Wren cautioned, "Let's have the hatch open first. He's a tricky customer; we don't want him trying to take us by surprise."

After Ellis had done as instructed, Wren glanced in and saw Ed Pushley lying on a mattress on one side of the cell. Pushley glanced up and gave Wren a dagger's drawn look, "What do you want?"

"Just want to talk," Wren replied.

Pushley snarled, "What about?"

Instead of answering Wren, glanced at Ellis and said, "Open the door but don't go away."

Overhearing the comment, Pushley laughed, "What's the matter Wren, scared of me, eh?"

He then rattled the short-chain cuffs holding him to a large D handle affixed to the cell wall. "Scared I might attack you?"

Ignoring the comment, Wren walked into the cell; glancing back at Ellis, he said, "If he tries to jump me don't hesitate to shoot him."

In response, Ellis pulled his stun gun out of its holster and ostentatiously set it to medium stun.

Satisfied he'd covered all bases, Wren plonked himself down on a chair not far from Pushley and then said, "So why did you try to kill us, Ed?"

"I was only after Mick Tarleton," Pushley replied.

Wren frowned, "Tarleton? You mean Mick Tarmy."

"Sorry," Pushley said, "Force of habit. When I first met him, he said his name was Mick Tarleton. He also calls himself Mick Tarmy."

"Okay," Wren replied, "Fair enough. Why are you after Mick Tarmy?"

The expression on Pushley's face changed; from being hostile, it became confused, "It's hard to explain."

"Try?"

Instead of supplying an answer, Pushley went quiet as if he was unsure why he was after Mick Tarmy. In an attempt to provoke a response, Wren said, "It isn't normal to want to kill someone without a good reason."

The confused look on Pushley's face suddenly changed to anger, and the way he spoke became very precise and clipped, "Mick Tarlton destroyed my operation, stole my money cards and made the Great Ones want to kill me. If I wasn't sharing Pushley's body, I would be dead."

Wren frowned, "Sharing Pushley's body?"

"That's what I've just said," Pushley snapped. "I'm now attached to Pushley."

Wren's frown increased, "If you are attached to Pushley, who are you?"

"I'm the spettro Mick Tarmy called Irrelevant."

Wren's frown increased but instead of challenging the comments that Pushley had just made he said, "I see."

Pushley said, "Tarmy destroyed my operation. I have good reason to hate him."

"What operation?"

"My orders were to invade Cittavecchia and arrest all the women archaeologists based there. I was also to take possession of a portable teleport when the shuttle landed. Tarmy prevented that happening."

"Arrest the women archaeologists. Why?"

"Because the Great Ones needed human women," Pushley replied.

"Why?"

"For their invasion program," Pushley revealed.

"Invasion program," Wren echoed. "What invasion program?"

"I'm surprised that Tarmy hasn't told you," Pushley said.

"Well he hasn't," Wren returned. "So why don't you tell me?"

There was a long hiatus, then Pushley said, "Okay. Over the

last few years, we have been sending female scientist home, er, how can I up it politely - we sent them home with an unexpected present."

"What sort of present?"

"A bun in the oven," Pushley said. "We sent them back pregnant with a spettro child."

Despite his violent past, Wren felt slightly nauseous. Although case hardened to indiscriminate killing, impregnating an unsuspecting woman with an alien life form seemed repugnant.

With anger rising, Wren snapped, "And why would you do that?"

"Normal spettri die if they leave the Fyfield Valley or the Altos Plateaux. However, the Great Ones realised a spettro foetus could survive a leaving if they are in a human womb. We have sent a large number of spettri to Arden that way."

Talking to himself, Wren said, "So that's where the prisoners in Minton Isolation Facility 1 came from."

Then to Pushley, "But a simple pregnancy test would highlight a woman's condition during the quarantine period."

"The spettro foetus forces its human host into embryonic diapause," Pushley replied.

"Embryonic diapause; what's that?"

"Delayed implantation," Pushley replied. "A spettro pregnancy can't be detected by normal methods. When a woman returns to Arden and finds herself pregnant, she presumes the pregnancy was the result of an encounter with someone after she's been released from quarantine."

"Who gave the orders to send the pregnant women to Arden?"

"The Great Ones, of course," Pushley replied, "My former masters."

Although Mick Tarmy had told him a great deal about his time in the Fyfield Valley, Wren still said, "Tell me about the Great Ones."

"They are the rulers of the Fyfield Valley and the Altos Plateaux," Pushley replied. "Soon they will be masters of the whole

Salus System."

"And how will they do that?"

"I've just told you that."

Wren said, "By sending pregnant women back to Arden with mutants inside them?"

Instead of answering, Pushley's demeanour and his normal voice returned; from being boastful, he became sullen, and he said, "You'll find out soon enough."

Ellis, who was still standing at the door cut in, "He's been like that ever since we put him in there. One moment he seems normal. The next his voice goes all weird, and he starts spouting stuff about the Great Ones; a real Jekyll and Hyde he is."

~*~

Alton Mygael glanced up from his desk and said, "I gather you've seen Ed Pushley."

When Wren nodded, he said, "Well?"

"Are you hoping that I will confirm what you already think," Wren replied. "That Pushley is a spettro?"

"Am I to take it that you don't think he's a spettro?"

"I didn't say that," Wren replied defensively, "Pushley actually said that he had a spettro attached to him. He said that the spettro was the one that Tarmy called Irrelevant."

"Then he's condemned by his own mouth," Mygael said.

"There is another alternative," Wren replied.

"And what's that?"

"The alternative is, Pushley is a nutty as a fruit cake," Wren replied.

Mygael sighed, "It's time to get off the fence, Allus. Is he a spettro or isn't he?"

"I'm not on the fence. Ellis described Pushley as Jekyll and Hyde. One moment he seems normal. The next his voice goes all weird, and he starts spouting stuff about the Great Ones."

"Based on what I've seen and the reports I've had from the guards," Mygael said. "I think he's possessed."

Wren half smiled, "What by? Irrelevant's evil spirit?"

"Yes," Mygael replied. "I've been giving the matter a great deal of thought. When I spoke to Mick Tarmy, he told me of an incident when he was with the spettro he called Irrelevant. Apparently, an Arcadian plesiosaur dragged this Irrelevant character out of an air-car and drowned him. A few days later, Pushley took Tarmy, Claire Hyndman and Nonie Tomio hostage. During that period, he spoke to Tarmy using Irrelevant's voice."

When Wren remained poker-faced, Mygael added, "Then Pushley came here and tried to kill us all by firing through the partition wall. If it hadn't been for the anti-stun paper lining the walls, we would probably all be dead."

Wren turned the question back on Mygael, "Is he a spettro or isn't he?"

"We have to presume he is a spettro," Mygael decided. "We then return to the same question. Do we hand him over to the police or keep him locked up?"

"It's illegal, but I say we keep him locked up," Wren replied. "Pushley will have to stay here until we teleport back to Arden. Once you resume your post on Arden, we can arrange to have Pushley moved to Minton Isolation Facility 1 and locked up with the other spettri."

"Good," Mygael said. "I'm glad we agree."

CHAPTER SIX

PUSHLEY REMOVES HIS HELMET AND WREN TAKES A GAMBLE

Arnold, the chief teleport controller, glanced up as Yalt clocked in, "Have you been in a fight?"

Not wishing to admit the truth, Yalt lied, "I just had a slight accident, padrone. I fell over against a stone wall."

"Well, make sure you clean yourself up before our customers arrive, you look terrible," Arnold chided.

He added, "Any chance of working an extra slot? We have an important consignment coming in later on."

Arnold opened up a power bubble and displayed the current teleport roster. He then pointed at the slot in question. Slots that occupied anti-social hours were very unpopular with most of the outworlders who were trained to work at the teleport facility. Being an Ab, Yalt usually drew the short straw.

"Well, can you do an extra slot?"

As Yalt was always short of money, he nodded and said, "Yes, padrone."

Arnold gave him a slight smile and passed him hardcopy details of the current slot. Two names leapt out of the sheet:

Alton Mygael and Allus Wren.

If the high priest had told him the truth, not only were these people responsible for imprisoning Ed Pushley; they were the

Great Ones' enemies. They were leaving Arcadia! What should he do?

Noting the alarmed expression on Yalt's face, Arnold growled, "Is there a problem?"

When Yalt shook his head, Arnold said, "Then go and set up. These people will arrive shortly. And like I just said, make sure you clean yourself up as well. You'll scare the hell out of them if they see you like that."

Yalt went straight to the teleport bay and began running through the standard check sequence. Once he'd finished, he followed Arnold's instructions, went to the comfort room and glanced in a mirror. As the washroom mirror had none of the imperfections of his home mirror, he realised why Arnold had been alarmed by his appearance; there were still streaks of blood on his face.

As he began washing away the remaining blood streaks, he mumbled, "I wonder what I should do about Alton Mygael and Allus Wren. Should I stop them leaving?"

His thoughts were interrupted when the mirror in front of him turned green. The high priest's image appeared and sent Yalt another mental message, "You will let Alton Mygael and Allus Wren leave."

"They are your enemies!"

"They are, but it is crucial to us that Ed Pushley escapes," the high priest replied.

"So, I let them go?" Yalt said.

"We can always deal with Alton Mygael and Allus Wren at a later date," the cleric replied. "Getting Ed Pushley off this planet has to be our priority."

When Yalt still looked worried, the high priest amplified, "Let them go. You will not do anything to hinder them. Ed Pushley's escape is vital to our plans."

~*~

There was a dull thud as the isolation helmet fell away and

hit the floor of his cell. Ed Pushley let out a sigh of relief. It had taken hours of dogged pulling and pushing before he'd finally removed the accursed helmet. Still, now he'd forced it off.

Exhausted from his exertions, he sank back in one corner of his cell and propped himself against the walls. While he was recovering, he felt something warm and sticky run down his neck and realised his ears were bleeding.

Reaching out, he grabbed some toilet paper and used it to staunch the bleed. The image of a man wearing ecclesiastical garb popped up in his mind. The occult symbols on his vestments and tall mitre hinted at unseen powers. Fearing the worst, Pushley made a grab for the isolation helmet. It might have taken him hours to finally force it off, but he couldn't take chances.

"No," the high priest's telepathic image shouted. "Don't put the helmet back on. You have nothing to fear from me. I am the bringer of good tidings."

When Pushley hesitated, the high priest added, "The Great Ones wish to speak with you."

Pushley was suspicious, "What about?"

"They would like to do a deal with you," the cleric replied.

Irrelevant's soul suddenly activated and instructed Pushley to respond with, "It wasn't so long ago the Great Ones condemned me to death. If I hadn't managed to transfer my essence into the body I now inhabit, I would be dead."

The high priest said, "We thought you had died. When the plesiosaurs dragged you under, your death seemed assured."

The high priest changed tack, "Can I say this? We were wrong to condemn you to death but stealing Ed Pushley's body and melding with him was a very clever response."

"Is that so?" Pushley replied icily.

Ignoring the sarcasm very evident in Pushley's thoughts, the cleric said, "It took us some time to realise what you'd done. That is why we have only contacted you now."

Irrelevant instructed Pushley to give the cleric another icy response, "I'm sure you haven't contacted me just to discuss old times. What do the Great Ones want?"

"I've told you. The Great Ones want to talk to you. They want to do a deal."

"Why?"

"Because they believe you could help them, of course."

Irrelevant instructed Pushley to say, "I was a slave who managed to throw off his bondage. Why would a free man volunteer to return to serfdom again, even if his freedom was only possible by co-owning another body? Why should I trust the Great Ones?"

The cleric said, "You won't be a slave or a serf. They want to offer you a genuine partnership."

"And why would they do that? What's the catch?"

The high priest's image developed a halo around it, indicating the remainder of their telepathic conversation was going to be held in private. "As you are aware, just before you escaped using Pushley's body, three of the Great Ones were killed in an explosion and another badly injured."

The cleric sent him images of an elaborate funeral procession staged to mark the triple passing. Lining the sides of a large cave complex were hundreds of the mutant humanoids. Most were standard long-jaw spettri, but there were also some very human-looking figures. There were even a few of the four-armed spettri lining the route.

There were twelve huge, six-legged Arcadian soldier wolves, leading the funeral cortege. Pushley noted their mandibles were wide open. Irrelevant whispered, "The open jaws signify the deaths of the Great Ones will be avenged."

Directly behind the huge soldiers, there were teams of smaller six-legged Arcadian worker wolves dragging three long draped trailers behind them.

As the sequence ended, Pushley asked, "What caused the explosion?"

"It was deliberate," the high priest said, "It was caused by a bomb."

Pushley was shocked. Although the spettro spirit sharing his body no longer worked for the Great Ones, old loyalties died hard. "A bomb! D'you know who was responsible for planting the bomb?"

"Yes. It was Mick Tarmy and his mistress, Claire Hyndman."

The comment made Pushley grind his teeth, "I hated Mick Tarmy and Claire Hyndman before I knew this. Now I've another reason to hate them."

Sensing he was winning the mental battle, the high priest added fuel to the flames, "Tarmy has also been involved in another attack on the Great Ones."

The first set of images was replaced by one showing the systematic destruction of one of the Zuka plantations that the Great Ones had built in the Fyfield Valley. As the sequence continued, the high priest added, "Although Tarmy did the dirty work, Walter Verex instigated it."

"Walter Verex? Never heard of him."

"Very few people have. He keeps a low profile," the cleric said. "Despite his power and wealth, he's a recluse. He hides away. He never appears in public. When he needs to engage with the outside world, he shields his real face behind computer-generated images. Despite his quirks, he's still the Principal Director of the Ingermann-Verex Corporation."

Pushley said, "Why are you telling me all this?"

"Because the Great Ones need your help," the high priest replied. "They also need to speak to you."

"If I speak to them, what do I get out of it?"

"If you agree to help," the cleric said. "You will be rewarded beyond your wildest dreams."

Irrelevant's spirit laughed, which created a smile on Pushley's lips. "That sound like something from an old Earth pantomime. Rewarded beyond your wildest dreams! Phooey! I need something tangible. I need a genuine offer. Money on the table."

Pushley then went into brag-mode, "When I escape from this planet, with my enhanced mental powers, being able to read minds, I will know what people are thinking and planning. I will also be able to discover their darkest secrets and blackmail them into co-operation. In short, I will be able to amass a fortune all by myself. I don't need the Great Ones' help."

"I have no doubt you will succeed in the short-term," the cleric agreed. "I have no doubt you will do very well while your luck holds out. Most clever or gifted people become very rich in places like Midway. But will you be able to keep your wealth?"

"What's that meant to mean?" Pushley snapped.

"Many men create great wealth, but most of them lose it again," The cleric replied. "This is because wealthy men swiftly develop powerful enemies who are determined to destroy them."

"And how and why would they do that?" Pushley challenged.

The high priest shrugged, "Sometimes, the dislike is caused by political conviction, but envy and spite are usually to blame. Given time you will develop enemies, and they will try to destroy you. The means of destruction are many."

"I'll take my chances," Pushley sneered.

"You could. But I wouldn't refuse our help if I was you," the cleric continued. "There is a saying - mud sticks."

"What mud?"

"Fake news, false accusations, trolling, abuse of legal powers, claims of sexual deviancy, your enemies will use any means they can to bring you down."

When Pushley remained silent, the high priest added, "The concept of not bearing false witness died out a long time ago. Your enemies will lie in court if they think they will get away with it."

When Pushley still didn't react, the cleric said, "But if you have the Great Ones working with you, watching your back, warning you of what your enemies are planning, you would not have to fear them. With the Great Ones' superior mental powers to assist you, they will be able to steer you clear of all the political rocks. You will be able to prevent your newly created kingdom from being attacked and destroyed."

"Newly created kingdom?"

"Wouldn't you like to be a king?"

"Of course," Pushley admitted. "But what do the Great Ones want in return?"

"What they have always wanted; to be able to escape from Arcadia and set up colonies throughout the Salus System and beyond if possible. They will go to places where they will be safe. You must realise that Arcadia is a dying planet. The Great Ones need to leave Arcadia before it's too late."

Irrelevant relented and instructed Pushley to take a chance. "All right, I will speak to them."

"Good," cleric said. "I will take you to see them."

Pushley frowned, "I'm locked up. How will you manage that?"

"I will transport you there mentally," the high priest said. A moment later, Pushley felt as if he was standing inside a massive cave.

The high priest said, "When the Great Ones emerge, keep your head bowed. Do not offend them. You will have much to lose if you do."

The image in Pushley's mind suddenly changed, and the high priest appeared to be standing not far from a large pool of still water. Behind that was a silver hedge-like structure. Beyond the hedge but virtually hidden by darkness, there were three tree-like objects.

Turning and bowing to his masters, the high priest began walking backwards, genuflecting every third step. Once he moved out of view, a ball of light emerged from one of the 'trees' and started flying over the pool. A second and third ball emerged from the other two structures and joined the first ball. Following the high priest's guidance, Pushley mentally lowered his head slightly in deference to their status.

The first ball sent Pushley a message, "Please accept our approbation. You have achieved a great deal in a very short time."

Irrelevant was surprised by the comment; Pushley spoke out loud, "What have I done?"

Instead of answering his question, the first ball sent him another message, "When your mission failed, we over-reacted. We hope you will forgive us because we forgive you. We now realise we sent you into battle badly prepared and ill-equipped for taking on such a powerful enemy. They had a military droid at their disposal, and you didn't."

Irrelevant/Pushley came back with, "The Great Ones are not in the habit of forgiving their underlings; failure is usually punishable by death. I, therefore, find what you are saying slightly unbelievable."

"The bombings have changed the Great Ones' outlook." the first ball said, "The three Great Ones who died were the hardliners. Now they are gone; it allows us to be more realistic. We now realise we are not omnipotent, and we need allies. We hope we can build a new partnership of trust with you."

"Partnership; what sort of partnership?"

"If you help us to escape, we will make you very rich."

This time instead of the vague promises made by the high priest, Pushley's mind began filling with the sort of pleasures that co-operation would bring in its wake. While images of beautiful women smiling down at him were still running through his mind, the first ball sent him another message. "Will you help us? You won't regret it."

When Pushley attempted to clear his perception of the alluring women and think logically, other images appeared. An attractive female chauffeur flashed up in his mind and opened an air-car door for him. Then rich men and women in suits began extending their hands in his direction and asking for a deal. As the clamour in his mind continued, money cards started dropping from the ceiling like ticker tape.

With the benefits of co-operation uppermost in his mind, Pushley accepted the Faustian pact. "Okay. We have a deal."

"Good. Once you have escaped, we will contact you again and agree on a full package that is acceptable to all parties."

Thinking that the interview was over, Pushley moved slightly, but the high priest checked him. "You are about to experience what very few other humans have experienced."

A moment later, Pushley was standing amongst a forest of

glowing trees. Glancing upwards, Pushley realised that he was now inside another colossal cave. He realised that some of the trees were moving and making way for him. One of the three balls of light appeared again and said, "Our people are not trees, Ed. The human mind is not powerful enough to comprehend what we are."

The high priest whispered, "When you reach Midway, you will need to replicate the conditions in this cave. We have already located several large warehouses with air-conditioning systems suitable for our purposes. Part of your remit will be to buy one of the warehouses and then teleport some of the Great Ones to Midway."

Pushley was about to start asking questions when the images vanished and he found himself back in his cell, chained to the wall.

Before he could descend into a deep depression again, the high priest re-appeared in his mind and said, "Your first objective is to escape from this cell."

~*~

Yalt recognised Mih Valanson the moment he walked into the teleport centre; he was the man who'd shot him. Catching a glimpse of Yalt, Valanson looked surprised, confirming Yalt's thoughts. But instead of confronting one another, they both remained silent. It was if they'd come to an unspoken understanding; it was water under the bridge. Yalt also knew that the high priest didn't want him to do anything to prevent Alton Mygael and Allus Wren leaving Arcadia.

Alton Mygael said, "Is everything ready?"

"I don't want you to go back," Klaien said in a pleading voice, "You know I think, it's a trap. Walter Verex is lying to you. Samantha hasn't been deactivated."

"Samantha has been deactivated," Alton Mygael replied, exasperation in his tone, "You know Walter Verex has confirmed Samantha has been deactivated. I have also spoken to several board members who've confirmed the same thing."

"Can't you see? It's a trap!" Klaien said. "They're all lying to you. Samantha has ordered them to say she's dead."

"Nonsense," Alton Mygael snapped. "I trust these people. Samantha's gone. I will have the board's support, and I won't be arrested if I return. I have to go back. It's my destiny, our destiny, that I reclaim my position now that Samantha has gone."

Mygael glanced at Wren and Philips. When they immediately came to attention, he said, "See - Zadernaster boys stick together."

He then began walking towards the teleport bay. Klaien looked at Wren, "Do it!"

He hesitated.

"Do it!"

This time, Wren complied. Slipping his stun gun out of its holster, he shot Alton Mygael in the back. As Mygael collapsed, Yalt tried to run off, but Mih Valanson grabbed hold of him and restrained him. Tam Philips moved in to assist and made sure he couldn't escape. Giving them both a wide-eyed look, Yalt said, "What is going on?"

Klaien walked over, "My partner wouldn't listen to reason. Don't worry; he's only stunned. Once he recovers, he probably won't even remember what happened."

Wren joined them, "We think he was about to teleport into a well-laid trap. So, we stopped him going."

When Yalt just stared at him open-mouthed, Wren spoke to Valanson. The other man handed him two cards, and Wren put them into his shirt pocket and then slipped on a head camera. He then nodded at Yalt, "Come on then - time for you to teleport me to Arden."

Yalt objected, "Three of you are supposed to teleport."

Wren patted his pocket and then glanced at Valanson. "I've been told these two cards will make the teleport indicate its transporting three people; namely, Alton Mygael, Tam Philips and myself… but I'm the only one going."

Yalt's face showed alarm, "If you go with those cards in

your pocket you could damage the teleport. You could also be killed."

"I'll take that risk," Wren replied. "Who wants to live forever?"

"Have you got your return ticket?" Klaien asked. Wren felt in another pocket for the boomerang device that Mih Valanson had manufactured for just this sort of eventuality.

After nodding, Wren stepped onto the teleport platform. As anticipated, the teleport confirmed it was transporting three people via one of the private space stations in orbit around Arcadia. Philips gave Yalt a nudge, "Do it."

Reluctantly, Yalt pressed a button. A moment later, Wren's body turned transparent and then disappeared from view.

CHAPTER SEVEN

A VISIT TO SAMANTHA'S LAIR, MINTON ISOLATION FACILITY 1

Three human outlines appeared in the teleport. Stu Othogon, the teleport controller at Minton Isolation Facility 1, knew that something was wrong. Glancing at the central control console, he let out a tut of disapproval because everything was shimmying alarmingly, and he could tell that his teleport system was busily wiping files. In an attempt to control the situation, he began issuing quiet verbal commands, but they were ignored.

As the shimmying grew worse, Othogon transferred his gaze to the teleport bay and tutted again.

Although it would only have been apparent to an experienced operator, he could tell that all three outlines materialising in the teleport were precisely the same. He was tempted to say something, but the squad of Black-Clads standing near to the teleport distracted him by coming to attention when Samantha came into view.

Othogon tutted again. It had been agreed that Samantha would remain hidden until Alton Mygael was arrested. Instead, she'd moved out of hiding so she could watch the spectacle unfolding. Like a *tricoteuse* waiting for the guillotine blade to fall, it was apparent she didn't want to miss anything.

Once out of hiding, Samantha whirred towards the teleport

bay. A few seconds later, one of the outlines hardened and Wren's body became visible.

When the other two shapes remained unaltered, Othogon realised his first instincts had been correct; two of the teleportees were dummies. "There's something wrong, ma'am."

Samantha shot him an icy look, "Wrong! What do you mean? Wrong!"

Othogon pointed at the images in the teleport bay, "It's a fake teleport ma'am."

Transferring her gaze back to the teleport bay, Samantha noted that Allus Wren's semi-developed image was smiling, seemingly amused by the situation. While she was still staring, Wren slipped one of his ghostly hands into his jacket pocket. A moment later, the three images in the teleport vanished.

"What's happened?"

"Wren must have been carrying a reversal device," Othogon replied.

Samantha snapped, "A reversal device!"

"Yes, ma'am," Othogon confirmed. "A boomerang device."

Samantha glanced at Nenet Khan, one of her senior officers and gave him a blinding look, "This should have been anticipated!"

Khan became defensive, "How could we have anticipated it, ma'am?"

"Because I equipped Claire Hyndman with a similar device during a previous operation," Samantha snapped. "It's obvious Wren worked out what I'd done and has used the same technology against us. When Wren returns, Alton Mygael will know I haven't been deactivated. Because of this stupid error, my plan has failed!"

Furious at being thwarted, Samantha's body began shaking, and her arms began flailing with annoyance.

Fearing for their lives, Khan and Othogon retreated to a safe distance. After twenty seconds, the shaking and the flailing stopped, and Samantha returned to normal. She immediately glanced at everyone clustered around the teleport bay, "You never saw Wren return. Understood?"

When they all just nodded, Samantha raised her voice a full decibel, "Is that understood?"

This time the whole group shouted back, "Yes ma'am; understood."

She then added, "And you never saw me shake - understood?"

Knowing what was expected, the whole group shouted back, "Yes, ma'am; understood."

"For the avoidance of doubt, "Samantha snapped. If anyone lets their tongue wag, I'll make sure they end up in a very nasty penal colony - is that understood?"

Once again, the whole group shouted back, "Yes, ma'am; understood."

~*~

"He's back!"

Klaien Mygael took a few steps towards the teleport bay and watched Wren's body reassemble. Once he'd become recognisable, Wren glanced in her direction and gave her a thumbs down sign.

Tam Philips said, "Looks like you were right ma'am. It was a trap."

Once Wren had completed his teleport Yalt moved in and led him towards the recovery area and went through the usual procedure, rest and food. Slumping back on a recovery couch, Wren glanced at Klaien, "Well, you were right. Walter Verex was lying. Samantha hasn't been deactivated."

"Are you absolutely positive?"

Wren removed the head camera he was wearing and set it on play. The power bubble image flickered a few times and then Samantha came into view, fury etched onto her electronic face. It was apparent she hadn't been retired as Walter Verex had promised.

Despite the seriousness of the situation, Wren smiled, "I bet she was really pissed off when I pushed the abort button."

Klaien returned the smile, "I bet she was."

Her face clouded slightly.

"What's up?" Wren asked. "Alton didn't fall into Samantha's clutches. That's what you wanted to avoid."

Klaien frowned, "Samantha's trap may have failed, but she'll still come after us."

"Valanson told me the cards, and the boomerang device, will have scrambled the teleport records," Wren replied.

"So, she can't come after us?"

"I didn't say that," Wren replied. "She may well try again."

He then sighed, "But right now, I don't want to think about Samantha. If you don't mind, we'll talk about contingency plans when I've recovered from the teleport."

Yalt intervened, "Mr Wren needs rest. What he did was very foolish. The devices he used has damaged the teleport. What he did could also have killed him."

Yalt's real worries then surfaced, "Who will pay to repair the teleport?

"How much damage has been done?"

Glancing at the teleport console, Yalt said, "I don't think it is severe, but it will take time to obtain spare parts."

Arnold, the chief teleport controller suddenly appeared, "What's going on?"

Sensing that Yalt's job was on the line, Klaien intervened, "This was entirely our fault. We disobeyed your technician's instructions. How much will it cost to repair?"

When Arnold told her, Klaien glanced at Alton's stunned body and said, "All things considered, that's a cost well worth paying."

Arnold gave her a harsh look, "What did you say?"

Wren cut in, "What she meant was, we apologise for what's happened, and we'll pay for the damage."

"Damn right, you will," The chief controller snapped, "You'll also pay for downtime and the lost revenues. Because of you, we can't teleport an important cargo."

Arnold then produced a device that looked like a small hair

drier and pointed it at Wren. The blood drained from his face, "Have you used a boomerang device before?"

"Why?"

"Because I'm getting incredibly high readings," Arnold replied. "So, I repeat, have you used a boomerang device before?"

When Wren nodded, Arnold said, "Come on, this is dangerous, we need to get him into a suspension unit."

Klaien looked alarmed, "Why?"

"Because if we don't, he's likely to fireball," Arnold snapped. "He's also likely to take this building with him."

Wren immediately thought about Stert Oryx. He'd flouted teleport rules, and his body had on gone into spontaneous combustion. There had been nothing left of him other than a pile of ash.

"Come on," Arnold chivvied. "We haven't much time."

As Yalt and Arnold dragged, Wren to his feet, Klaien said, "How long will he have to remain in suspension?"

Arnold let out a hollow laugh, "How long is a piece of string?"

"What do you mean?"

"He's probably going end up in suspension for anything from three to six months," Arnold replied. Once Wren was alongside the nearest suspension unit, Arnold pointed at a plastimetal bowl. He said, "Empty your pockets into that."

As Wren complied, he glanced at Klaien and said, "Take my percom and make sure you call Mick Tarmy. Tell him what has happened."

"You said you didn't have a Mick Tarmy's contact details," Klaien said.

"Well, I do," Wren said as they loaded him into the suspension unit, "Contact him."

A moment later, Arnold slammed the unit shut, and it immediately kicked in.

Arnold moved forwards, menacingly, "Right, that's one problem solved," and grabbed Wren's percom.

Klaien objected, "I have to make an urgent call."

"Tough," Arnold snapped. "This could contain vital evidence."

He then passed the percom over to three uniformed security guards who'd just walked in, stun guns raised.

Glancing at Arnold, Klaien said, "What's going on?"

Arnold glared at her, "What's going on!"

Pointing at Alton Mygael, Arnold added, "Someone has been shot, and the teleport system has been damaged."

"I said that we'd pay for the damage," Klaien replied.

"I've no doubt you will," Arnold replied. "You'll also pay for looking after Mr Wren while he's in the suspension unit."

Klaien looked that the security guards, "Why are they here?"

"You have endangered life and broken teleport regulations," Arnold snapped. He then added, "Might I suggest you get yourself a lawyer, you'll need one."

He then gave Yalt an icy look, "You're suspended until further notice. Now get out of my sight."

CHAPTER EIGHT

PUSHLEY ESCAPES FROM HIS CELL

P ushley began working on his handcuffs linking him to a stout plastimetal bracket on one wall. Eventually, bruised and bleeding, he managed to slide his hand out. He let out a deep sigh of satisfaction. Now he could escape and take up the Great Ones' offer.

~*~

Rundle Levan beckoned to Ben Ellis. Once Ellis was close enough, Levan lifted the shiny plastimetal lid off the tray that Ellis was carrying. After swiftly inspecting the food, Levan said, "Have to make sure there are no files or saws hidden in there, don't we?"

Ellis rolled his eyes; Levan said virtually the same thing every time their paths crossed.

With the inspection over, Levan said, "I'd come up with you, but I'm not feeling too well. Had a bad night. I've had the trots, and I've got pains all over. Must be coming down with something."

"No worries," Ellis said and began climbing the external fire escape that gave access to the mid-floor of the main building. Partway up, Levan called out, "Be careful. Pushley's in a strange mood again."

"I'm used to his strange moods," Ellis called back.

"Yeah," Levan said, "But Pushley knows that Klaien Mygael and the rest of 'em have been arrested. He also knows Allus Wren is in a suspension unit."

"How does he know that?"

Levan shrugged, "Nobody told him. Maybe he can read our minds. Be careful."

"Quit worrying," Ellis called back. "I know how to handle Pushley."

Once at the top of the stairs, Ellis turned toward the cells. Five paces later, his eyes misted over, and he staggered against a wall.

He vaguely heard Levan call out, "You okay, Ben?"

Recovering Ellis shouted back, "I'm fine," but after walking another six steps, he staggered again. Then something began moving around inside his skull, and he began to have flashbacks. Some of them were from his early childhood, while others were recent.

With more and more images racing through his mind, Ellis staggered again, and a voice said, "Don't put the tray through the hatch. Open the door."

Glancing around, Ellis wondered where the voice had come from.

"Open the door."

Ellis's mind swam again, and he nearly dropped the tray.

"Put the tray down on the floor and open the door."

Walking the remaining distance towards the cell, Ellis placed the tray on the floor. He then reached for the bunch of keys, he kept suspend from a belt loop and found the one that fitted Pushley's cell. He inserted it in the lock even though he knew he was supposed to have a backup before opening the cell door.

"Open the door."

Instead of complying, Ellis fought back.

"Open the door."

With Pushley urging him on, Ellis eventually turned the key. The tumblers had barely clicked to open before the heavy door sprang back and smashed Ellis out of the way. Then Pushley threw himself across the landing and made a dive for the stun pistol Ellis was carrying in a hip holster.

Realising he'd made a bad mistake, Ellis rolled sideways in an attempt to prevent Pushley taking his weapon. As they were struggling, Ellis's mind filled with more of Pushley's demands, "Give me the gun."

More struggling, "Give me the gun."

As the fight continued, Ellis found himself succumbing to the energy emanating from the escaped prisoner. He felt his gun being ripped from its holster as Pushley forced him into submission.

Climbing to his feet, Pushley aimed the stun gun at its former owner. But instead of firing Pushley bent down, grabbed hold of the handcuffs Ellis had hanging on his police duty belt and told the guard to roll over. Once Ellis had complied, Pushley cuffed him before he had a chance to struggle. Ordering Ellis to his feet, Pushley prodded him in the back with the gun, making him move down the corridor towards the fire escape.

Before they reached the door, Pushley had a change of plan and told his prisoner to halt. He grabbed Ellis's percom and punched a number.

Impatient for an answer, Pushley mumbled, "Come on, come on, Yalt. Come on, come on, damn you!"

Just as he about to repeat the mantra, Yalt answered. Pushley snapped, "Have you still got the ground-van?"

"Yes," Yalt replied. "I am driving it now. I was waiting for you to contact me."

"Where are you now?"

"Lyndon."

"Where's that?"

"Not very far from Alton Mygael's house."

"Excellent," Pushley purred, "Then get out to Alton Mygael's house fast. I need you to pick me up where you dropped me off. Understand?"

"Yes, padrone."

"How long will it take you?" Pushley snapped.

"The road is bumpy," Yalt replied. "but I am not far away. I will be very soon."

Although Pushley would have preferred a more precise answer, he said, "Make sure you are very soon, Yalt."

He picked up on some of Yalt's stray thoughts and Hal Warmers' image formed in his mind. Sensing Yalt might betray him, Pushley added, "And don't tell Hal Warmers you've spoken to me or that you are coming to pick me up. Understood?"

He snapped, "If you betray me to Warmers, I will personally impale you on a spike in the town square."

To back up his threat, Pushley sent Yalt some horrific mental images. Yalt's mind responded as Pushley had anticipated; it waved a white flag and capitulated.

Satisfied that Yalt would remain on-side, Pushley slipped the percom into a top pocket and frisked Ellis for any hidden weapons. While searching, he found Ellis's wallet. As it had money cards in it, he dropped it into another of his pockets.

Once he was satisfied that Ellis couldn't cause him any trouble, Pushley began propelling the other man down the corridor again.

Reaching the external door, Pushley told Ellis to step out onto the fire escape landing. As he did so, Levan glanced up. Realising Pushley was free, Levan made a threatening gesture with his gun. As killing a guard would make him a wanted criminal, Pushley flipped to medium stun and took Levan down. He told Ellis to walk down the staircase.

Once they had reached ground level, Pushley turned Ellis into a human shield and forced him to walk crabwise towards the nearest door in the external perimeter wall.

More out of defiance than belief, Ellis said, "You won't escape."

"You'd better hope I do," Pushley replied. "If I die, I'll make sure you do too. Now keep walking."

He then activated Ellis's percom again, flipped it to open frequency and contacted the guard in the nearest watchtower. "I'm leaving, and Ellis is coming with me. If anyone tries to get in the way, Ellis dies."

When the tower guard lowered his rifle, Pushley knew he'd won the battle of wills but just to be sure he raised his gun. Although it was a long-distance shot, the guard crumpled. Satisfied he'd subdued local opposition, Pushley forced Ellis to keep on walking towards the external gate. Once alongside it, Pushley placed the stun gun against Ellis's forehead. "Try to be clever, and you're a dead man."

He held the percom in front of Ellis's mouth, "Tell them to open the gate."

Fearing the worst, Ellis did as instructed. A moment later there was a distinct click as the gate opened and Pushley told Ellis to step through it.

Within seconds, several armed guards appeared, but Pushley called out, "Stay back or Ellis dies."

To reinforce his threat, Pushley raised his gun against Ellis's temple once more and said, "Place your guns on the floor, or he dies."

Instead of doing as instructed the guards began glancing at one another wondering if they should comply with the demand. Taking advantage of their indecision, Pushley flicked his gun from kill to heavy stun and sprayed the area in front of him. As the guards collapsed, en-mass, Pushley gave Ellis another shove, "Start walking again."

Knowing it wouldn't be long before other guards appeared, Pushley forced Ellis into the surrounding woods and began moving towards his rendezvous point. They'd barely made thirty meters before Pushley heard excited voices close by; the hue and cry had started.

Not wishing to be caught, Pushley gave Ellis another shove and said, "Move."

As they moved deeper into the wood, they passed an irrigation ditch; mosquitoes rose up and came swarming in. Ellis began complaining, "I'm being bitten to death."

Pushley brought the butt of his pistol down on one of Ellis's shoulders and snapped, "If you don't keep your mouth shut, I'll stun you and leave you to drown in the ditch."

Guessing that Pushley wasn't bluffing, Ellis fell silent even though he could hear the remnants of the security force crashing through the woods searching for the fugitive. When the crashing sounds grew closer, Pushley realised that it wouldn't be long before they found him, and he went on the attack. He locked onto the mind of one of his pursuers and began using his mental powers to spread seeds of disinformation. Two seconds later, he heard the man shout out, "I can see him. He's over there."

Thinking his ploy had backfired, Pushley glanced back, when he saw figures racing off in another direction, he realised his mental intervention had worked. To make sure, he locked onto another guard and gave him the same treatment. There was another shout, and all the guards began running faster, running in the wrong direction.

Pushley let out a slight chuckle, gave Ellis a shove and said, "I've only just realised just how powerful my mind is and just how easy it is to force humans to do my bidding. It's child's play."

He began to brag, "When I arrive on Midway, inducing fools to finance my plans will be a walk in the park. With the mental powers I possess, I can't lose, especially if I have the Great Ones to help me."

Hearing the sound of an approaching ground-van, Pushley propelled Ellis forward again until they finally reached a secluded clearing. A moment later, Yalt trundled into view in his cousin's battered ground-van.

Noting Yalt was wearing a beaded hat Pushley asked, "What's with the hat? Don't you trust me?"

"I always wear a hat," Yalt protested.

Letting the hat issue lie, Pushley bundled Ellis into the ground-van's cab and then leapt in next to him pushing him closer to Yalt. Once he'd slammed the door, Pushley shouted: "Get away from here fast."

As Yalt moved off, doing his best to avoid the worst of the

potholes in the rutted track, Pushley snapped, "I said fast."

Yalt gave Pushley a worried look, "I will do my best padrone, but the road is not good here. If I damage the ground-van you won't get very far, will you?"

While the ground-van bounced and wobbled on its way, Pushley saw an air-car high above. Although there was no indication that the flying machine had located them, Pushley realised it would only be a matter of time before Alton Mygael set up roadblocks to prevent him from escaping.

Noting Pushley's worried looks, Ellis predicted, "You won't escape. I'd surrender while you can, if they start shooting, you could wind up dead."

Ignoring Ellis, Pushley said, "Is there any other way out of here?"

Yalt's eyes rolled, "There may be another way, but it could be dangerous."

"What way?"

"There is an old tunnel not far from here, but it was abandoned many years ago."

"Where does it go?"

"It cuts through the mountains; there is a road on the other side that leads to Awis town."

"Why was it abandoned?"

Yalt pointed at the air-car searching for them, "There is little need for tunnels anymore. Your people don't use ground cars or ground-vans."

Glancing up at the circling air-car, Pushley realised that attempting to escape via the most obvious route wouldn't work. They'd either be forced to surrender or killed before they went half a kilometre. "Is the tunnel safe?"

Yalt shrugged. "It's been years since I've been there. I'm not sure what condition it is in, padrone."

"I've seen that tunnel," Ellis cut in. "It's boarded up because it's unsafe. If you go down the tunnel, you'll kill us all."

Ignoring Ellis's doomsday predictions, Pushley made the only obvious choice, "Okay. Let's try the tunnel."

"You're both mad," Ellis yelped.

Ignoring Ellis's interjection, Pushley repeated his instruction and Yalt set off down a side track. As it was less rutted than the area outside Alton Mygael's house, the ground-van was able to pick up speed. Glancing around, Pushley noted that the road they were taking was surrounded by large trees and palm plantations. As there were water-filled irrigation ditches on both sides, Pushley realised the locals had learned to push back the surrounding desert by pumping water out of the lakes.

Pushley glanced upwards and let out a sigh of relief. With the trees spreading their boughs and palm leaves over the entire road, it was unlikely that the prowling air-car would see them passing by below.

Ten minutes later, the tunnel entrance loomed up. As predicted the front of the tunnel had been roughly boarded over. Pushley glanced at Yalt, "Have you got a rope?"

When Yalt nodded, Pushley kept his gun levelled at Ellis. "Okay, Yalt get the rope and attach one end to the bull bars on the front of the ground-van and tie the other end to the timbers covering the tunnel entrance."

When Yalt returned, roping completed, Pushley told him to reverse the ground-car. Within seconds the boarding collapsed, leaving the tunnel entrance gaping open. The tunnel was surprisingly short, with light visible at the other end; it was evident that the other side wasn't boarded.

Pushley glanced at Ellis, "Have you got a head torch in your equipment pack?"

"Why?"

"Because when I send you into that tunnel, you are less likely to fall over if you have a head torch."

"Send me into the tunnel! Why?"

"Simple," Pushley replied. "If you can get through on foot, we should be able to drive through in the ground-van. So, have you got a head torch?"

Instead of answering, Ellis just scowled.

Clicking the stun gun to kill, Pushley prodded Ellis's head,

"Have you got a head torch?"

Fearing death, Ellis nodded. On finding the head-torch, Pushley jammed it onto the other man's head. After turning the torch on, Pushley opened his door, slid to the ground and told Ellis to get out. Once Ellis had done as instructed, Pushley pointed at the tunnel and said, "Right - unless you want me to shoot, start walking."

With reluctance written all over his face, Ellis began walking into the tunnel.

After making sure that Ellis carried on walking, Pushley turned to Yalt and pointed the shattered timbers, "You'll have to clear that away."

Without a quibble, Yalt climbed out, cleared away the debris and retrieved the rope. By the time he'd finished, Ellis had reached the end of the tunnel.

Pushley made his assessment, "It looks clear."

Climbing back into the ground-van, he called out, "Come on, Yalt let's do it."

Yalt scampered back, leapt behind the wheel, restarted the engine, flipped on the headlights and then drove into the end of the tunnel.

As the small vehicle began to inch forwards, Pushley sensed he'd made the correct decision. Although some debris had fallen from the tunnel arch, there were no heavy falls, nothing to prevent the ground-van from making progress.

Once they emerged at the other end, Pushley instinctively glanced upwards and was pleased to note no air-cars were prowling around overhead.

Glancing at Ellis, Pushley decided to take no chances and stunned him. As the other man collapsed into an untidy heap, Pushley glanced at Yalt and said, "I need you to get me to the teleport centre."

"The teleport centre is damaged, padrone," Yalt replied.

"Damaged!" Pushley echoed, "How?"

Yalt's face fell, "Because things happened."

"What things?"

Yalt began telling Pushley about the cards and the boomerang device Allus Wren had used. He then became whiney, "Even if the teleport was working, going to the teleport centre would be very dangerous for you, padrone."

Despite Yalt's protective hat, Pushley picked up on some of Yalt's stray thoughts. As Hal Warmers' image formed again, Pushley snapped, "Have you been talking to Warmers?"

"No padrone. I did not tell him about coming here," Yalt replied. "But after I left you here and went back to Awis town the other time, he found me. He says you owe him money. I have no doubt he's having the teleport centre watched."

"How long will the teleport centre be closed?"

Yalt shrugged, "I do not know. Maybe a short time but I cannot guarantee it. Sometimes it takes many days before spare parts come. The spare parts only come when the main supply air-vans visit Awis or by special delivery."

Pushley said, "So I can't use the local teleport for the foreseeable future? And Hal Warmers is still after me?"

"Yes, padrone."

Thinking fast, Pushley added, "Is the safe house I was using still available?"

"Yes, padrone."

"Then I will stay there until I can work out what to do," Pushley replied and opened Ellis's wallet. Finding a low-value money card, he handed it to Yalt. "You're working for me again. Understood?"

Yalt grabbed it; as the teleport facility was down and he wasn't being paid, he needed every penny he could get.

Pushley repeated himself. "You're working for me again. Understood?"

Yalt said, "Yes, padrone. I am working for you again."

Despite the hat Yalt was wearing, Pushley detected loyalty emanating from his Ab associate. "Good, do I have your promise you won't betray me?"

"I won't betray you, padrone," Yalt said. "I promise."

Waving a hand in the direction of Awis town, Pushley said,

"Okay, take me back to the safe house."

When they finally reached the outskirts of Awis town, Pushley ducked down. He only sat up again when Yalt drove the ground-van down a narrow access way and into a small yard at the back of the safe house.

Once inside, Pushley moved around the rooms, gun at the ready. Satisfied there no one waiting to ambush him, he began pulling down the blinds in the principal rooms to protect him from prying eyes.

He glanced at Yalt, "You are telling me the truth, aren't you? Hal Warmers doesn't know I'm here."

Yalt said, "I promise you, padrone. I have not told Mr Warmers anything."

Satisfied, Pushley added, "I need you to get me some food. I also need a disguise and some hair dye so no one will recognise me when I go out. You got me a good disguise last time I was here, but I need something different. Understand?"

When Yalt nodded, Pushley gave him some more money cards and said, "Don't speak to Warmers."

"I won't padrone," Yalt promised.

Once Yalt had left, Pushley went upstairs, had a shower and found a first aid kit to dress the abrasions he'd suffered during his escape. He lay down on his bed. The high priest re-entered his mind almost immediately and said, "Congratulations, Ed. You succeeded in escaping. As discussed, I need you to go to Midway."

"What's so special about Midway?"

"The spettri we sent to Arden have all been arrested. It would be too risky to send you there."

"But why Midway?" Pushley pursued.

"Midway is the most powerful planet state in the Salus System," The cleric said. "If we gain control of Midway, all the other human colonies will swiftly fall to us. Besides, we have scores to settle on Midway. When you reach Midway, this man is one of your assignments."

The high priest then sent him a fuzzy image that had obviously been taken by paparazzi through a darkened car window.

Despite the high priest's status, Pushley couldn't disguise his contempt, "With an image like that how am I expected to locate him? Who is he?"

"I have already told you about him," The high priest replied. "His name is Walter Verex; the Principal Director of the Ingermann-Verex Corporation; the man who instigated the destruction of one of the Zuka plantations the Great Ones had built in the Fyfield Valley."

"So, you want me to go after Verex," Pushley replied, "Then what?"

"Verex is important," the high priest intoned. "But the most important objective is to obtain a warehouse and teleport facilities for the Great Ones. Once you have proven your loyalty, you will start receiving your rewards."

"Okay," Pushley said, "Once I've organised a warehouse and teleport, how do I punish Verex?"

"You kill him," the cleric said.

"And if I succeed in killing Verex, I will be rewarded?"

"Handsomely."

Thinking of his unfinished business on Arcadia, Pushley said, "What about Mick Tarmy and his two witches: Claire and Nonie? And what about Alton Mygael?"

"They have made other enemies," the high priest replied. "When we are ready, we will ensure that Alton Mygael's enemies find him. Mick Tarmy will suffer the same fate. But not yet."

"Why not yet?"

"Because I will not be diverted by side issues," the cleric replied. "My principal aim is to start evacuating the Great Ones as soon as possible. Once that has successfully been accomplished, we can then set about pruning the deadwood, namely Alton Mygael and Mick Tarmy."

When Pushley didn't reply, the high priest said, "I also intend to make sure you do not allow yourself to be distracted from the most important matters."

Once the cleric's image had evaporated from his mind, Pushley swore.

Hearing the blasphemy, Yalt said, "What is the matter, padrone?"

"Everything!" Pushley snapped. "Life!"

When Yalt gave him a rather alarmed look, Pushley sighed, "Mick Tarmy stole a bag full of money cards from me. The high priest wants me to forget the money and go to Midway."

He then added, "And how am I supposed to escape to Midway with the teleport system down?"

The high priest suddenly popped up in Pushley's mind again, "Awis Oasis is not the only place with a teleport system. You know that only too well. You have also proven you can force most humans to comply with your will. There is another teleport facility in New Melbourne."

"And how am I supposed to get there?"

"You are not thinking things through," the high priest chided. "With your mental powers, you could easily steal an air-car and force the guards on Awis's gates to let you through."

From being depressed, Pushley's thoughts took wings. "You are right. I can get out of here."

"Make sure you reward Yalt for his help," the cleric said. "You will also take Yalt with you when you leave."

Pushley's jaw dropped, "Why should I take Yalt with me?"

Instead of admitting that he found mind linking with Yalt extremely easy, even when he was wearing his hat, the high priest said: "Because he is trustworthy and speaks the local languages."

The cleric added, "If you follow my advice, you will escape from Awis Oasis. Once you have, you will also realise that with our help you can achieve a great deal."

Unhappy with the way the high priest had left their previous conversation, Pushley said, "Who are these enemies going after Mick Tarmy and Alton Mygael?"

"Who d'you think?"

Pushley snapped back, "I'm not in the mood for guessing games. Who are these enemies? The ones who will deal with Mick Tarmy and Alton Mygael. Tell me!"

"Samantha! The humanoid who controls Arden," The high priest said.

"Samantha," Pushley echoed. "Why should Samantha want to kill Mick Tarmy and Alton Mygael?"

The high priest's image in Pushley's mind said, "Because Mick Tarmy and Alton Mygael know too much about her activities. I have no doubt it will not be long before she decides to have a spring clean."

When Pushley's thoughts indicated he was sceptical, the cleric added, "As Samantha is a droid, neither the Great Ones nor I can enter her mind. But the Great Ones have monitored her human staff, analysed her previous actions and have built up a profile. They believe that when her power is challenged, Samantha will squander resources relentlessly pursuing her political opponents. Logically, she will pursue Alton Mygael and Mick Tarmy until they are dead. The Great Ones' military resources are limited, so they have decided to step aside and let Samantha deal with Alton Mygael and Mick Tarmy."

Pushley cursed, "Tarmy stole a bag containing a small fortune in money cards from me, and I want it back."

"Correction," The cleric replied. "He stole our bag containing a small fortune in money cards, but we are prepared to move on."

When Pushley pulled a face, the high priest added, "I said, we are prepared to move on. And so, must you."

CHAPTER NINE

ED PUSHLEY LEAVES AWIS OASIS

Klaien Mygael gave the two police officers a hostile look, "How long are you going to keep me here?"

"That largely depends on you," one of the officers replied.

"I've told you everything."

"So, let's go through it again," Officer One said. "You asked Allus Wren, who is now in suspension recovering from the teleport accident to shoot your life partner to prevent him teleporting to Arden."

"Yes," Klaien replied. "Why do we keep on going over the same ground."

"We just want to be sure we understand what you're telling us," the second officer

said. "So, let's go through it again…"

~*~

"How long are they going to keep me here?" Klaien said.

Berclay Narden shrugged, "I don't think they believe you."

"Good lawyer, you are," Klaien griped. "You're supposed to be on my side."

"I am on your side," Narden replied. "But this business about a rogue droid, the one you call Samantha…"

"What about Samantha?"

"The local police have made enquiries with the Ardenese authorities. They have been told that Samantha does not exist and never has existed."

"That's nonsense," Klaien snapped. "Samantha was my life partners deputy. When

Alton comes around; he'll tell them that."

"Alton has come around," Narden replied. "Unfortunately, he hasn't been of much help. He can't remember very much at the moment."

"Eh?"

"I understand that his condition isn't uncommon," Narden replied. "The stun ballast he took was a medium stun, not a minimum stun. For a man of Alton's age, it will take his system some time to recover."

"So where does that leave me?"

"The police believe you tried to have your life partner murdered. Most murders and attempted murders are committed by partners, close relatives and family friends."

"Well, I didn't try to kill Alton," Klaien insisted. "The others will tell you that."

"Oh! They have," Narden confirmed. "But the police still believe they are dealing with attempted murder."

When Klaien went silent, Narden said, "One piece of good news."

He then held up Wren's percom, "You wanted this."

He then said, "Be quick. I've got to hand it back. I'll be back in five minutes."

"How did you get hold of it?"

"How d'you think?" Narden replied. "Around here, the only way of getting anything is by bribery. But I didn't say that. Lawyers aren't supposed to do things like that, are they?"

"Will they take a bribe to let me out of here?"

"I'm working on it," Narden replied. "But if I manage to swing it, the bribe will have to be substantial. You're a big fish. The police like arresting high profile figures, it's good for their media ratings."

He then pointed at Wren's percom, "You've got five minutes."

Once Narden had left the interview room, Klaien swiftly interrogated Wren's percom and then contacted Mick Tarmy.

The response was not favourable, "How did you get this number?"

"Listen. Don't hang up! This is important," Klaien said, "Samantha has not been deactivated. Walter Verex went back on his word."

"Samantha hasn't been deactivated?" Tarmy quizzed. "How do you know?"

"Wren teleported back and saw her," Klaien said. "He managed to boomerang back."

She then said, "One of the security guards came to visit me. Ed Pushley has escaped."

"How did he do that?"

"I don't know," Klaien admitted.

"Has he left Awis?"

"We don't think so," Klaien admitted. "We have people searching for him, but there are plenty of places to hide in Awis town."

"Thanks for letting me know," Tarmy replied.

"Is that it?" Klaien demanded. "Aren't you going to do something?"

"Yes," Tarmy said. "I am going to do something. I'm going to send two A10s back to the tower. With luck, the A10s will be able to track him. And like I said, thank you for letting me know."

"Good," Klaien said, "One last thing, don't call me back on this number. I won't be able to answer. I've been arrested."

~*~

Pushley glanced at Yalt. "What's this?"

"It's a monk's habit," Yalt replied.

"Where did you get it?"

"I found it," Yalt replied. "It was hanging on a line."

Pushley snorted, "What you mean is, you stole it?"

"Yes, padrone."

"You want me to dress as a monk?"

"Nobody challenges monks," Yalt said. "You will be safe walking around wearing that."

Pushley grimaced, "Monks are nothing more than a bunch of scroungers and parasites."

"You may think this," Yalt explained, "but they are respected in Awis. They are men of God. If you wear a habit, you are unlikely to be challenged. If you don't want Mr Warmers to find you and kill you, dressing as a monk is the best way."

After a lot of thought, Pushley pulled the habit on. He then glanced at Yalt, "So, what d'you think? Will I pass muster?"

"Yes, padrone. You will be okay," Yalt said. "You look like a real monk."

"And how will that help me?"

"You will be able to walk around outside," Yalt replied.

"I don't want to walk around outside," Pushley snapped. "I need some money, and I need to get out of Awis."

"This will help, padrone," Yalt said and held out a large bowl.

"What's this for?"

"It's an alms bowl, padrone," Yalt explained. "Real monks beg for alms."

"You want me to go begging?"

"Real monks make a lot of money begging," Yalt told him.

"A lot of money?"

"Yes, padrone."

"Where did you get the alms bowl?"

"I found that too," Yalt replied, and then beefed up his previous comments, "Even the poor put money into the alms bowls of monks. They put in money and then ask the monk for a blessing."

Pushley said, "What sort of blessing?"

Once he'd learned the phrases in the local dialect, Pushley said, "So if I dressed as a monk, people would fill the bowl with lots of money?"

"Yes, padrone."

A slight smile formed on Pushley's lips, "Okay, I'll give it a go."

He then picked up an apple that Yalt had bought in the market, took a bite out of it and then glanced at the bottle of hair dye, "Give me an hour to get ready and then we'll go out."

~*~

"Good," Pushley said, "Now you know what you have to do?"

"Yes, padrone," Yalt replied. "Find a suitable air-car."

He looked hopeful.

Knowing what was required, Pushley handed over some low denomination money cards.

As Yalt pocketed the money cards, he said, "I will have to see my brother first."

"Why?" Pushley demanded.

"Because if you want me to leave Awis with you," Yalt said. "I have to give him some money to tide him over until I return."

"Okay," Pushley agreed. "But once you have spoken to him find me a suitable air-car. I'll meet you back here in an hour. I'm going to see if this begging bowl of yours works."

As Pushley began walking away, Yalt set off towards his house. Once there, he presented his brother with the money cards that Pushley had just given him. He explained that he had to leave and then set off to towards one of the local car parks.

~*~

Once he neared the centre of Awis town, Pushley adjusted the monk's habit making sure the cowl obscured his face and began walking towards the centre. The market was thronging with people, mainly wealthy tourists who'd flown across the desert as part of their package tour.

Checking his habit was correctly adjusted, Pushley moved deeper into the market with his alms bowl held out in front of him. Without prompting, people all around began placing money cards, and coins into his alms bowl; Pushley recited verbatim what Yalt had taught him.

Walking further into the market, Pushley eyed up one group of tourists and moved in on them. He then began mind-probing, a predator looking for a suitable victim.

"How much?" a loud voice said. "Aw, come on, do me a deal."

Attracted by the hectoring tones, Pushley moved forward. A moment later, Pushley saw the fat wallet stuffed into the other man's back pocket.

Moving closer, Pushley used his mental powers to induce Loud Mouth's friends to turn away. Once they had, he mentally demanded Loud Mouth's wallet. For a second or two, Loud Mouth resisted Pushley's mental demands. Then, he succumbed, pulled the wallet out of his pocket and dropped it into the begging bowl as Pushley walked by.

Pushley responded by saying the words that Yalt had taught him again. He added, "Thank you for your generosity kind sir; you will be rewarded in heaven."

Keeping Loud Mouth in a trance, Pushley moved away and swiftly lost himself in the thronging masses. He walked well away from the scene of the crime and found a suitable place to count his booty. After removing Loud Mouth's ID and pocketing all of the money cards and small change, Pushley dropped the empty wallet into a litter bin.

He was about to return to the fray when Loud Mouth suddenly came out of the trance, realised he'd been fleeced and began screaming, "I've been robbed. I've been robbed."

When the shouting grew louder, Pushley moved away from the market realising that to do otherwise would be pushing his luck. Once he was well clear, a slight smile formed on Pushley's face, "That was easy; so easy. I demanded that guy's wallet, and he just handed it over."

Twenty minutes later, he met up with Yalt again. "Well? Have you found a suitable air-car?"

"It is difficult padrone," Yalt whinged. "All the air-cars are security protected."

"Meaning that you haven't been able to find anything suitable?"

"No padrone."

Pushley let out a sigh of disappointment and was tempted to demand his money cards back. Instead, he said, "I shouldn't have sent a boy to do a man's job. Take me to where you have looked."

Yalt took the lead, and five minutes later, they arrived at a small car park. Telling Yalt to stand guard at one of the entrances, Pushley moved to a convenient point and leaned against a wall. He then dropped his head so that the cowl obscured his features in its shadow.

Five minutes later, a man strode into view. As he was wearing a well-cut suit and making his way towards a top of the range air-car, everything about him suggested importance. Smart Man was also brandishing his key fob in one hand; it made him an easy target. Without moving a muscle, Pushley entered Smart Man's mind and began probing for information. A look of surprise briefly appeared on Smart Man's face only to be replaced by a vacant stare as Pushley's powerful mind overwhelmed him. After probing for a few seconds, Pushley said, "Bingo. Come on, Yalt This guy can get us out of here."

Moving towards Smart Man, Pushley added, "We've just struck gold, Yalt. This guy is called Toni Felado, one of Awis Oasis's richest and most influential men. He's a multi-millionaire."

Pushley waved to Yalt, urging him to follow, "Come on."

Once Yalt had joined him, Pushley told him to get into the back of the air-car. Instead of doing as instructed, Yalt just stared at Felado who still had a completely blank expression on his face.

Giving Yalt a nudge Pushley said, "Get in the back."

Once Yalt had done as instructed, Pushley climbed in the other side and was pleased to note the rear windows were darkened glass. A moment later, the high priest made his presence felt, "Well done. Tell Felado you want to go to New Melbourne."

Once Felado had climbed in, Pushley followed the high

priest's instruction. In response, Felado told the air-car to fly to New Melbourne via the South Gate.

Staring at Felado's expressionless face, Yalt said, "You're controlling him, aren't you, padrone?"

"Of course," Pushley replied casually, and then moved forwards and began rifling through his victim's pockets. Finding Felado's cardholder, Pushley glanced inside it. Although the photograph on Felado's ID card was nothing like Pushley, he still placed in his top pocket.

Yalt gave him a sharp look, "Why have you taken his ID padrone?"

"Arcadia is virtually a droid free planet; security checks are made by humans," Pushley explained, "With my mental powers, I should be able to make the security guards believe the ID is mine or yours."

He found some high-value money cards, removed them and then placed the empty cardholder back into one of Felado's pockets.

When Yalt gave him another sharp look, Pushley justified his actions by saying, "We need money if we are to survive Yalt, and Felado's a rich man. I'm sure he won't miss what I've taken. I'm also certain he's well insured. People like him always are."

As a sop, Pushley pushed a few coins and low denomination money card into one of Yalt's pockets. When the Ab didn't refuse them, Pushley smiled, "I thought you'd come around to my way of thinking."

As they neared the South Gate, Pushley whispered, "Slide down. I don't want the guards to see us."

Yalt and Pushley moved out of sight. When the air-car came to a halt, Felado depressed a speaker and told the guard that he had to go to a business meeting in New Victoria. Recognising him, the guard responded by opening the outer gate.

Once the air-car was through, Pushley said, "See that? Felado is a respected citizen; the guard didn't bother to check to see if there were any passengers."

As the air-car surged forwards into the gloom of Arcadia's

long night, headlights blazing, Pushley let out a sigh of relief, "We've done it, Yalt! We've escaped from Awis Oasis!"

~*~

Felado's air-car was immediately detected by the two A10s Mick Tarmy had stationed at the survivor tower. One of the A10s set off in pursuit but made no attempt to attack the fleeing vehicle. Instead, it began stalking, taking photographs whenever it could.

CHAPTER TEN

PUSHLEY'S SOJOURN AT BOTTLE CREEK

When Pushley swore out loud, Yalt gave him a worried look, "Is something the matter, padrone?"

Pushley swore again, "Yes. I can feel my mental powers fading."

He'd barely spoken before Felado opened his eyes and came out of his trance-like state. He then realised he wasn't alone. "Who the hell are you two? What are you doing in my air-car?"

In response, Pushley smiled disarmingly, "We're just hitchhikers, and you kindly offered us take us to New Melbourne. You fell asleep, but I'm sure you must remember."

Felado opened his jacket and displayed a holstered gun, "Bullshit, I never give hitchhikers a lift. We're going to land, and you two are getting out."

Pushley glanced out of the air-car at the desert below, "You can't just dump us in the middle of nowhere."

Felado's hand closed around the butt of his gun, but before he could draw, Pushley beat him to it and threatened him with his stun gun. After disarming Felado, Pushley said, "I'm afraid we're staying. New Melbourne here we come."

Ignoring the stun-gun, Felado said, "Hijacking is a serious offence."

"We're not hijackers," Pushley replied. "We both distinctly heard you offer us a lift."

He then gave Yalt a nudge, "My friend here has an excellent memory. I'm sure he'll confirm we are just innocent hitch-hikers and you kindly offered to take us to New Melbourne."

Nudging Yalt again, Pushley added, "Isn't that right?"

Picking up on the second prompt, Yalt nodded, "Yes padrone. We are just innocent hitch-hikers, and this kind man said he'd take us to New Melbourne."

Felado gave Pushley an icy look, "Okay smart arse, if you're innocent hitch-hikers, why are you pointing a gun at me?"

"You started it!" Pushley replied. "You tried to pull a gun on us. We just want to make sure you don't go back on your word."

Felado glared at him and then glanced away. Despite his thought-fade, Pushley still realised his reluctant host had just triggered some sort of emergency sequence. A moment later the air-car began changing course.

Without commenting, Pushley shot Felado in one arm. He then said, "Cancel the alarm and put us back on course."

Instead of complying, Felado looked shocked, "You've shot me."

"And I'll shoot you again if you don't cancel the alarm and put us back on course," Pushley replied. He aimed at Felado's other arm.

Before he fired, Felado caved in. "No, don't shoot - I'll do what you say." He added, "The controller is in my pocket."

With gun levelled, Pushley told Yalt to find the device. Once Yalt had located it, Pushley snapped, "So what do we do to cancel?"

With Pushley's gun under his nose, Felado provided the cancellation code. A moment later the air-car went back to its original course.

"Good," Pushley said, "If you try any more tricks, you're a dead man."

Pushley picked up on more of Felado's thoughts and realised the air-car was still emitting distress calls.

Waving the stun gun under Felado's nose again, Pushley told him to cancel the alarm, but the other man shook his head and a smug expression formed on his face, "I can't. Once the distress calls are triggered, they carry on transmitting until a specialist turns them off. It's designed to prevent hijackers, like you, from forcing their victims to turn the system off."

"Turn it off!"

"I've just told you," Felado replied. "I can't."

Pushley became agitated and began waving his gun at Felado menacingly, "You'd better find a way."

Although Felado looked scared, he still dared to say, "If you kill me, the police will throw the book at you; for first-degree murder, hijacking and robbery. You'll be lucky if you don't get a forty to fifty-year stretch, even a death sentence. In New Victoria, the relatives of the murdered person can determine the form of execution. It's part of the constitution."

When Pushley paled, Felado added, "The last murderer executed in New Victoria died on a gibbet. No one thought the court would authorise it, but they did. Do you fancy swinging by your neck until the life is choked out of you? They tell me it's a very nasty way of dying."

Pushley waved his gun at Felado again and snapped, "Shut your mouth and turn the transmissions off."

"I've told you. I can't."

Pushley was still thinking about what he could do to force Felado into revoking the alarm when he began picking up on thoughts coming from afar. He realised that police air-cars were already locked onto their position and were closing in. Realising his bid for freedom was about to wind up in calamity, Pushley began probing Felado's mind searching for a solution, but none was provided.

Realising he was running out of time, Pushley's mind went into total meltdown. There had to be a way out, but he couldn't find one!

The high priest's image suddenly popped up in Pushley's mind and then linked with Felado's as well.

A few seconds later, Felado began talking in a language that Pushley didn't understand. Within seconds, the air-car banked sharply and increased speed. Realising the cleric had succeeded where he hadn't, Pushley said, "What's happening?"

"Felado could cancel the alarm in his own language," The cleric replied. "However, the police don't appear to be giving up the chase. They are still on an intercept course."

When Pushley swore out loud again, the high priest said, "Fear not! All is under control. There is nothing for you to worry about."

"You said the police were still closing in," Pushley snapped, still waving his gun at Felado.

"I have told you," the cleric replied. "All is under control. I can't prevent the local police from intercepting you if you maintain your present course. However, the police aren't allowed to pursue you over a state border. The air-car has now been reprogrammed to take you to Bottle Creek, Zeelandia."

Pushley let out a long sigh of relief. Bottle Creek was about eighty kilometres over the border; even overzealous NV police officers were unlikely to trespass that far into the territory of a neighbouring state.

While Pushley was still recovering, the high priest added, "While you were stationed at Fort Saunders, you made several short trips to Bottle Creek. I hope you have friends there and will be well received."

"I have, and I will be," Pushley predicted, "I know a lot of people there. You couldn't have chosen a better bolt hole. Thank you."

"Which proves my point," the high priest said. "If you team up with us, we can protect your back."

"Point taken," Pushley replied. "But a visit to Bottle Creek wasn't exactly on my itinerary."

"You will still need to go to New Melbourne to teleport," the cleric said, "but if you stay at Bottle Creek for a few days until the dust settles, you should be able to go there without any trouble."

Glancing at Felado, Pushley said, "Not much chance of that if he makes a statement to the police, and they post us as wanted criminals."

"Once you reach Bottle Creek," the cleric said, "I will instruct Felado to fly back to Awis Oasis. No doubt the police will intercept him, but Felado won't remember anything. On the way back, he will forget all about you and Yalt."

"And how will you do that?" Pushley jibbed. "How can you guarantee Felado will forget about the hijack?"

"We are skilled in such matters," the high priest said. "You needn't worry. By the time the police intercept Felado's car, he will remember nothing concerning you or the hijack. He won't be able to describe either of you."

The cleric then added, "A word of warning, Tarmy has had a droid following your air-car ever since you left Awis Oasis."

Frightened, Pushley began glancing in all directions, "Where is it?"

"I can't give you it's the exact location," the high priest said. "But reading the minds of Tarmy's associates leads me to believe, it is following at a discreet distance."

Pushley went pale, "D'you think that Tarmy will instruct it to kill me?"

"I cannot read Tarmy's mind," the cleric admitted. "When we try, we are bombarded with images of bombings and mass-killings."

Irrelevant's soul whispered, "I have had the same trouble with Tarmy."

Pushley said, "So you don't know his intentions?"

"I am afraid not. But don't worry," the high priest said, "Once you reach Bottle Creek, I will ensure the air-car lands close to one of the main buildings so you can dash inside."

He added, "It would be sensible if you kept undercover while you are at Bottle Creek. The droid may have instructions to kill you."

A few minutes later, Felado's air-car touched down. Once Pushley and Yalt had climbed out, they both raced towards the nearest door and found themselves inside a large meeting hall.

Pushley moved towards a nearby window, eased back a corner of a curtain and glanced out. As dawn had broken, he was able to look around. He let out a sigh of relief when he couldn't see a droid lurking around nearby. He transferred his gaze to Felado's air-car. Felado was still sitting inside, totally blank-faced.

The high priest, whispered, "Do not worry, the mind-wipe is working. Very shortly, Felado will remember nothing about the last few hours."

While Pushley was mentally thanking the high priest, Yalt said, "Where are we, padrone?"

"We are amongst friends," Pushley replied.

As if to confirm the statement, Glyfin Fenmor came barging through an internal door and strode into the hall to greet Pushley. As he closed the distance, Fenmor boomed out, "Ed, what are you doing here?"

He looked at the monk's habit that Pushley was wearing, "Why are you dressed like that? Last time we met, you said you had no time for organised religion. Surely you haven't taken holy orders?"

"It's a long story," Pushley replied dismissively, "I had an accident, damaged my clothes, and this was the only thing I could get in my size."

He began working on Fenmor's mind to force him into a change of topic.

After shaking hands with Glyfin Fenmor, Pushley introduced Yalt. In response, Fenmor said, "So why are you here, Ed? Is there a problem?"

Noting the mild suspicion in Fenmor's tone, Pushley shrugged, "Just a flying visit. Nothing to worry about."

He then invented a half-truth, "We're trying to get to New Melbourne, but we had to divert. Technical problems."

Sensing more questions forming in Fenmor's mind, Pushley squashed them. Then, without prompting, Fenmor said, "I'm flying to New Melbourne in a few days. I can take you with me if you like."

Pushley smiled, "Perfect."

"Well, I'd better find you some quarters while you're waiting," Fenmor said, making for the outer door.

Fearing Tarmy's droid, Pushley began to panic, but swiftly regained composure when the high priest whispered, "Tarmy was forced to withdraw the droid."

"Forced to withdraw the droid," Pushley echoed. "Why?"

"You know the answer to that," the cleric replied.

"Do I?"

"Arcadia is a POSSI, a planet of special scientific interest," the high priest reminded him, "Droids are banned from most POSSIs. It's a rule designed to prevent mining companies from moving in heavy robotic mining equipment and destroying evidence of First Empire settlements in the process."

"I still don't understand," Pushley bleated. "Why was Tarmy forced to withdraw his droid?"

"The police alert also attracted the attention of one of the enforcement satellites. It instigated an anti-droid sweep of Bottle Creek," the cleric explained. "Tarmy had to withdraw his droid before it was detected and destroyed."

"So Tarmy can't come after me," Pushley said. "If he does, there is a strong possibility that his droid will fry."

"Correct."

"When I go to New Melbourne," Pushley said, "Will Tarmy be able to use this droid against me there?"

"New Melbourne, like most of the major illegal colonies, has a permanent anti-droid sweep," the high priest said.

Pushley's fears began to evaporate. "So Tarmy is unlikely to be able to use his droid against me while I am Bottle Creek, when I'm on my way to New Melbourne or once I'm in the city."

"Correct," the cleric replied. "In short, I would say you have little to fear from Tarmy."

While Pushley was still thinking about what he'd been told, Fenmor called out, "Come on."

Pushley stepped out and followed. After walking the best part of a hundred metres, Fenmor pointed at a large tent, "I'm afraid we'll have to put you up in this for a few days."

~*~

Once Fenmor had left, Pushley glanced around the tent and sniffed; although it was large, more like a yurt than a conventional tent, Pushley was not impressed. "I may have served in the army, but I still don't like roughing it."

As Yalt had lived in a squat for his whole life, he just shrugged, "It will do padrone. We ought to be thankful Glyfin Fenmor provided us with a roof over our heads."

Pushley decided to be more diplomatic, "I suppose you're right. As Glyfin Fenmor has provided shelter, and offered transport to New Melbourne, I suppose we can't complain."

Pushley glanced at his watch and then at the tent flap. Although dawn had arrived and Arcadia's long day had started, he felt drained. Glancing at Yalt, he said, "The last few hours have been very stressful, Yalt. I'm going to grab some shut-eye, make sure I'm not disturbed."

As Yalt was aware that outworlders were forced to day-sleep because they were not used to Arcadia's long day/night cycle, he nodded; "Yes, padrone. I will make sure you are not disturbed."

"Good man," Pushley replied and then collapsed onto his allotted camp bed. Before he had a chance to fall asleep, he found himself mind linking again, but this time it wasn't with the high priest.

Almost immediately, Mick Tarmy's image flashed up in his mind. He then saw Claire Hyndman and Nonie Tomio. Closing his eyes and relaxing his mind, Pushley began probing deeper. After attempting to mind-link with Tarmy and Hyndman and being rejected, Pushley concentrated on Nonie Tomio. While he was still probing her mind, the name Moxstroma's Nursery emerged.

Leaping out of bed, Pushley grabbed his percom and searched for the name he'd just seen. A few seconds later, a location plan and a detailed description of the nursery appeared. Pushley let out a whoop, "We've got 'em."

Yalt frowned, "What is it, padrone? Got who?"

"I've just discovered where Mick Tarmy, Claire Hyndman and Nonie Tomio are hiding."

Yalt said, "Why are these people of interest to you, padrone?"

"These people have caused me a great deal of trouble," Pushley replied.

"So, you intend to punish them, padrone," Yalt speculated.

Pushley shook his head, "No. Given half a chance, I intend to kill 'em."

Yalt frowned, "Are you going to tell the high priest about your plans?"

"No," Pushley snapped. "And neither are you!"

Yalt went very quiet for a while and then said, "The high priest is very clever; he may read my mind and force me to tell him about your plans."

Pushley reacted by grabbing hold of Yalt's hat and slamming it onto the other man's head. "He won't be able to see your deep thoughts if you wear your hat, now will he?"

"What if he suspects you are up to something and asks me directly, am I to lie to him?"

"Yes, you'll lie to him, damn it," Pushley snapped. "I'm going after Mick Tarmy, Claire Hyndman and Nonie Tomio, and I'm going to teach them a lesson they will never forget."

Yalt went quiet again and then said, "If you tell me why you hate them much, padrone, I will consider your request."

"Consider my request!!!!"

Yalt cringed but stood his ground, "Yes, padrone. The high priest is mighty; I will be taking a great risk if I do as you ask me."

It was Pushley's turn to go quiet.

Eventually, Yalt repeated himself, "You must tell me why you hate them much."

Irrelevant took over Pushley's mind entirely and spoke through his host's lips. "The Great Ones gave me a vital job to do, and Tarmy, Hyndman and Tomio thwarted me. By doing so, they made me an outcast and stole my money. That's three reasons for hating them. Is that enough or do you want more?"

Yalt thought about what he'd just been told and then said, "How much money did they steal, padrone?"

Pushley was tempted to tell Yalt that the bag contained thirty million Eron dollars but checked his tongue. If Yalt knew how much was involved, he'd get greedy. Instead, Pushley said, "It was a great deal of money. More than you could understand. So, is that a good enough reason?"

"Yes, padrone."

"So, you'll keep your trap shut then?"

"Trap?"

"Your mouth," Pushley snapped, "Keep your mouth shut. No snitching or telling tales to the high priest."

"I will keep your trust, padrone," Yalt agreed, even though there was a frown grooved into his forehead.

"Good," Pushley said, "So now, I'm going back to bed. If you're around, make sure I'm not disturbed."

With that, he moved back to the camp bed, lay down again and within seconds, sleep claimed him.

Although the outside temperature had started to rise, Yalt moved towards him and placed a thin blanket around Pushley's shoulders. He was about to walk away when Pushley shouted out, "No! No! No! Don't let the plesiosaur kill me," threw the blanket to one side and hurled himself off the camp bed, arms flailing as if he was trying to swim.

Thinking he'd caused the outburst, Yalt became apologetic, "I'm sorry, padrone."

Pushley glanced up at Yalt and said, "It wasn't your fault. I had a bad dream."

Although the high priest had already told Yalt about Irrelevant's death, and how he'd been killed by an Arcadian plesiosaur, he pretended that he didn't know.

"About a plesiosaur," Yalt hazarded.

Pushley nodded, "How did you know?"

"You called out, don't let the plesiosaur kill me," Yalt revealed.

Pushley shivered; dying by being dragged underwater had become a recurring dream for him. Although it had been the spettro that Tarmy had dubbed Irrelevant who'd been pulled underwater and taken in a death roll by the plesiosaur, Pushley often had drowning nightmares.

The bad dreams were a confirmation that Pushley had become a dichotomous being. Irrelevant might have died in the Fyfield River, but he'd escaped real death by attaching his mental energy to a part of Pushley's brain; he'd become a parasite.

"Why, why were you dreaming about a plesiosaur?" Yalt quizzed.

Not wishing to tell Yalt too much, Pushley clammed up, "I've no idea. Dreams are dreams. Who knows where they come from? Who knows what they are really about?"

When Yalt nodded in agreement, Pushley said, "I'll be okay. Why don't you go and see if you can get something to eat?"

"Are you sure you'll be okay?"

"I just had a bad dream," Pushley assured him. He added, "If you are coming with me to New Melbourne, go get a haircut."

Yalt half turned, but instead of walking off he said, "Once we've been flown out of here, do you intend to go after Tarmy, Hyndman and Tomio?"

Pushley shook his head. "I've been thinking about that. If I go after Tarmy and his people, he will use his droid against us. He has a TK5 they call Alex, it's an ex-military droid, and it's armed with a phaser and has invisibility cloaks."

"You are a spettro."

"Even spettri can't mind control droids."

Yalt let out a sigh of relief, "So you've changed your mind. You are going to forget about Mick Tarmy."

"No," Pushley replied. "I'd be a fool if I attempted to go after them. So, I'm going to force them to come after me."

Yalt was tempted to ask how Pushley intended to force Tarmy into coming to him, but he let the question slip. The less he knew, the better.

Once Yalt had left the tent, Pushley remade his bed and the

lay down again. He resisted the temptation to sleep because he knew the drowning nightmare would probably return. Instead, he cleared his mind and began trawling the ether. Eventually, he mind-linked with Nonie Tomio again.

After looking through her eyes, listening through her ears, Pushley sensed she was in a hotel. Her mind filled in the blanks; the farmhouse at the nursery was uninhabitable.

He discovered she was alone and unlikely to be disturbed. After a little more probing, a slight smile formed on Pushley's lips. Tarmy was with Claire Hyndman.

CHAPTER ELEVEN
PUSHLEY'S KA VISITS NONIE

Nonie awoke with a start. Although she knew that a new day had dawned, the room she was in seemed very dark. Worse, she could see something moving out of the corner of her eye but was scared to turn her head to see what was there.

Her mind began to race. There definitely something moving in one corner of the room. Or was there? Maybe it was just her imagination?

Despite her analytical thoughts, she remained frozen, unable to move. A few seconds later, the shadow doubled in size and moved closer to her bed. Eventually, the silhouette underwent a metamorphosis and developed depth and colour. A moment later, a face appeared.

Ed Pushley gave Nonie a none too friendly smile, "Do you remember me, Nonie?"

Still frozen with fear, Nonie didn't respond, but she remembered Pushley only too well. During the time they'd been stationed at Fort Saunders together, Pushley had shown her a great deal of interest. However, it swiftly became apparent his interest was purely physical. He'd just wanted a quick lay; a co-operative woman to lie in his bed.

When she'd refused his overtures, her appraisals dropped from A to D within a matter of weeks. Small errors of judgement were swiftly magnified to make her appear incompetent.

Oh! Yes. She remembered Ed Pushley only too well. Not only was his face etched in her mind, there no mistaking his plummy Midwain accent and supercilious attitude.

"What's the matter, Nonie?" Pushley purred. "Cat got your tongue?"

Instead of answering, Nonie attempted to pull the bed covers over her face; an ostrich response, but her arms refused to co-operate.

Her mind began to race again. It then started looking for comparables. A few seconds later, she unearthed forgotten memories. When she was a child, the jockey had been her worst nightmare. The bareback rider lived in a cupboard in her room. His favourite trick was jumping on her in the middle of the night.

After having its fun, the jockey left as silently as it came. Of course, Nonie knew her unwanted rider didn't exist. The jockey had been some sort of hallucination.

The knowledge brought her strength. Although Pushley had appeared to be in her room, she knew he wasn't really there. What she was seeing was just a bad dream. Or, if it was real, given time, Pushley would grow bored with the game he was playing, and like the jockey, he'd just disappear.

Pushley's ka moved closer, "So where's Mick, your lover boy, eh? He's with Claire tonight, is he?"

Still frozen, Nonie remained silent.

Getting no response, Pushley said, "You don't believe I'm here, do you?"

Still getting no response, Pushley slipped one hand beneath the bedclothes and grabbed hold of one of her breasts. The ice-cold contact broke the spell, and she recoiled.

Pushley started laughing, "I thought that would get your attention. Can't beat a bit of physical contact, can you?"

He ran his hand down her body, and referred to their time at Fort Saunders, "We never really did get to know one another properly, did we, Nonie? I always thought that was a great shame."

Sensing where Pushley's hand would end up next, Nonie

pulled away again and snapped, "Get off me, you perv."

When Pushley just smiled, Nonie glared at him, "This is not funny!"

"No, it's more educational," he replied. "I didn't realise I could experience physical contact in an out of body state. Now I realise I can. Most educational. No doubt I'll be able to have hours of fun in the future."

"What, sneaking up on sleeping women and feeling them up," Nonie snapped.

Pushley grinned, "Why not? With every day that goes by, my mental powers grow in strength."

Nonie's mind went back into overdrive. Pushley had more or less confirmed that Mick Tarmy's theories were correct. Somehow, Pushley had managed to change from a normal human being into a spettro.

She thought about his last claim. If it wasn't just a brag, very soon Pushley would be unstoppable.

Reading her thoughts, Pushley said, "I am not a spettro in the real sense of the word, my dear, but I do now possess most of the powers of a spettro. If my powers continue to grow soon, I will be unstoppable."

Breathing deeply in an attempt to control her fears, Nonie gasped, "What d'you want, Pushley?"

"Just a quiet chat," Pushley replied. "For now, that is."

He smiled again, "Why are you sleeping alone?"

Nonie bridled, "What's it to you?"

"Mick is sleeping with Claire," Pushley observed. "Is this man swapping a regular thing or has the ménage à trois fallen apart?

"The what?"

"Ménage à trois," Pushley replied. He then explained, "When three people are in a permanent relationship."

"What's wrong with that?"

Pushley shrugged, "I've always found that relationships develop and then crumble very quickly. Then again, I'm used to commune living. Most commune relationships are transient in my experience. So, I'm curious. Can a permanent relationship between three people really last for long? Take you, for instance. I'm wondering if Claire Hyndman has won the day, and you and Mick Tarmy are now past history?"

Piqued by the comments, Nonie snapped, "I'm happy with the way things are."

"So, you haven't broken up with Mick Tarmy."

Losing her temper again, Nonie snapped, "Neither Claire nor myself have left Mick. We're still partners. So, other than prying into my private life, what d'you want Pushley?"

"I've told you, a little chat. For now."

"And what if I don't want to chat?"

In response, Pushley hit her mind like a sledgehammer and mentally transported her back to the time she'd been trapped on the small convoy in the middle of the Fyfield River. While she was reliving the experience, she saw several Arcadian millipedes swimming towards the boats.

Even though she knew that Pushley had done something to her mind, Nonie reacted by grabbing an imaginary boat hook and slashing at the millipedes to prevent them from climbing on board.

After playing with her for a minute or so, Pushley brought her back, "As you seem to have a short memory Nonie, I thought I'd remind you of my mental powers. Which are immense."

He mentally transported her back to the Fyfield River again, and she found herself hanging over the side of an inflatable boat. Glancing sideways, she saw Claire Hyndman in a similar position with the waves making her splutter each time one washed over her mouth.

"I could have killed you when I had you, prisoner," Pushley said. "I'd stunned both you and Claire Hyndman."

He added, "If I'd pushed you into the water as I'd been tempted, you would have both have drowned."

To prove his point, Pushley then created a simulated drowning in her mind, and Nonie felt as if her lungs were filling with river water. He then brought her out spluttering and said, "I do hope that demonstration will convince you of my power. I can kill you anytime I want to, Nonie."

He simulated the drowning in her mind again. As he finally allowed her to gain her breath, Pushley said, "I made you feel like you were drowning again, just to prove the point, Nonie. If you don't do what I want, I will kill you. Do you understand?"

While Nonie was still gasping for breath, Pushley said, "I didn't hear you, Nonie. Do you understand?"

This time Nonie nodded, "Yes. I understand."

"Good," Pushley replied. "I want the bag with the money cards in."

"Alex has the bag," Nonie replied. "It's inside his safe. I will never get it off him."

Pushley swore and then went silent for nearly twenty seconds. Eventually, he said, "Then you will come to me. You will become my hostage. It will be interesting to see what Tarmy does. Will he part with the money or let you die?"

Nonie began to panic, "Why are you doing this?"

"I want the money, and I want revenge," Pushley said. "And if I don't get what I want I'm going to kill you. Do you want me to kill you?"

Not getting the answer he wanted, Pushley began simulating the drowning feeling again. He watched, dispassionately, while she flailed her arms, gasping for air.

Just as she was on the point of passing out, he released her lungs from his mental vice and waited while she gasped for air. He said, "I want the bag with the money cards in, and you are going to help me get them back. Do you agree?"

"Yes, yes, yes," Nonie gasped. "I agree. I'll do what you want."

"Good," Pushley replied. "But if you let me down, I will kill you."

A moment later, his shadow left the room, and the light from the window streamed in.

For a second or two, she thought it had all been a dream, but then she noticed bruising on one of her breasts. As the bruise was vaguely hand-shaped, she realised it hadn't been a nightmare. Ed Pushley had made a visitation.

CHAPTER TWELVE

PUSHLEY HEADS FOR NEW MELBOURNE

E d Pushley glanced at himself in the mirror and frowned. Although beggars shouldn't be choosers, Pushley still sniffed; the clothes he'd been given to replace the monk's habit were olive drab army surplus.

He was about to turn and leave his tent when the mirror turned green, very nearly matching the colour of the uniform he was wearing, and the high priest's image replaced his own. "I understand you are leaving for New Melbourne today."

"That's the plan," Pushley confirmed. "I'm not sure exactly when. I'm waiting for Glyfin Fenmor's call."

"Good," the high priest replied. "Once you reach New Melbourne, I will try to organise your teleport to Midway as promptly as possible."

Pushley frowned, "Is there a problem?"

"Since we last communicated, I have discovered the local teleport is booked solid for months in advance," the cleric replied. "We can only hope someone will cancel and provide you with a slot."

"So how long am I likely to be kicking my heels in New Melbourne?"

"With luck only a few days. Then again, it might be a few weeks," the high priest said.

"A few weeks!"

"That's a worst-case scenario," the cleric replied. "If that happens, I will arrange some additional funding. We can't have you starving, now can we?"

"And when I get to Midway. What then?" Pushley said.

"We have already discussed this," The cleric snapped. "When you arrive, you will organise the mobile teleports. One will be set up at your end; the other sent to the Fyfield Valley."

"Once that is done, we will need a large warehouse either to buy or with a long-term lease. We have already located three suitable warehouses with atmospheric control suitable for the Great Ones to live in. Once you have secured a warehouse, some of the Great Ones will be sent to Midway."

"What then?"

Then you will be free to start phase three," the cleric replied. "You will locate and kill Walter Verex."

"And what if I get caught?"

"You are worrying too much," the high priest said. "With our assistance, you will not be troubled by the local police."

"I worry too much, do I?" Pushley snapped back and began dredging up possible problems. "If what I've seen on the movies is correct, most big cities on Midway have banks of CCTV cameras in most public places. Most of the cameras are equipped with facial recognition systems. If something goes wrong, the local police will have no difficulty arresting me."

"We will provide you with diplomatic override cards," the high priest said, "I will ensure someone will be waiting at the teleport centre when you get there. They will give them to you."

"And what exactly are those?"

"They are what they say they are," the high priest said, "If you are carrying one, the local camera systems in New Melbourne and the teleport system will respect your diplomatic immunity."

"More importantly, when you arrive on Midway, most of the security systems will also recognise your diplomatic status and leave you alone."

"You said most," Pushley pointed out. "What about the ones that don't."

"You are correct," the cleric replied. "In high-security areas, you will be picked up, but high-security areas are signposted with power bubbles so that you can avoid them."

When Pushley still looked uncertain, the cleric added, "You have the powers of a spettro, Ed. No one on Midway will be expecting your arrival or the strength of your mental abilities. You will be able to carry out all phases of the operation with ease."

"Is it absolutely necessary to kill Walter Verex?" Pushley said.

"Yes," the high priest said, "The deaths of the fallen Great Ones must be avenged. Besides, with your mental powers, you will be able to kill Walter Verex with the greatest of ease and make it look like an accidental death."

"If it's so easy," Pushley snapped. "Why haven't your people already killed him?"

"Even our mental powers are taxed when we attempt to mind-link with people living on Midway. But if you were there, your mental strength would be immense."

"I could also wind up in prison if I get caught," Pushley replied icily. "Or worse, shot dead by the police."

"That won't happen," the cleric assured him. "We will help you all the way. It's in our interests that you escape and remain on station. We have been trying to place an active spettro either on Arden or Midway for years. You are now our best chance."

"And if I do what you ask, I will receive all the benefits promised," Pushley said.

"Of course. The Great Ones have already discussed this with you. You will be well rewarded," the high priest replied.

"How long do you think it will be before you can, organise a teleport slot to Midway?" Pushley asked.

I have already told you, the high priest said, "With luck only a few days. Then again, it might be a few weeks."

"I presume you will have no objections if I take in the sights while I'm waiting," Pushley said.

"Of course. Enjoy!" the cleric replied and then disappeared from Pushley's mind.

Yalt said, "Is there something the matter padrone?"

Turning towards the tent's entrance, Pushley saw Yalt standing in the doorway and said, "No ... nothing important."

"You were speaking to the high priest," Yalt observed, "He wants you to go to Midway to help the Great Ones escape and kill the man called Walter Verex."

"That's his plan," Pushley confirmed, "But as I told you, I have some unfinished business on Arcadia. I have to lure Mick Tarmy, Claire Hyndman and Nonie Tomio into a trap. I know they are not far from here. I just have to get them to where I want them, and I think I know exactly how to do that."

"How?"

"There is no need for you to know," Pushley said, tapped the side of his nose. "I don't want you going blabbing to the high priest."

Yalt shrugged, "Then don't tell me then. It doesn't matter to me. It's probably better that I don't know."

"My sentiments entirely," Pushley countered.

Yalt changed tack, "Why do you want to kill Mick Tarmy, Claire Hyndman and Nonie Tomio?"

Pushley said, "Mick Tarmy destroyed my plan and made me an outcast. The Great Ones might have forgiven me, but I have no intention of forgiving Tarmy, Hyndman and Tomio; they are going to be punished."

Pushley added, "I have another reason for wanting to find Tarmy. He has something that belongs to me. If I recover my bag with the money cards inside it, I won't need to go to Midway. I'll be able to tell the high priest to get lost."

"What happens if you don't get your money back?" Yalt said. "Or, what if Mick Tarmy has spent your money?"

Pushley was tempted to tell Yalt about Tarmy's fear of using the cards and the amount of money involved but checked his tongue. If Yalt knew the full facts, he'd get greedy. Instead, Pushley said, "I think it's unlikely."

"If you don't get your bag back," Yalt said. "Will you go to Midway?"

Pushley considered, "If I don't get the bag back, I suppose I'll have to."

"If you do go to Midway, what happens to me?" Yalt said. "I am an Ab; I am not allowed to leave this planet."

Pushley extracted several low denomination money cards from his wallet and gave them to Yalt, "Don't worry; if I have to go, I will give you enough credit to get back to Awis Oasis and money to live on; I will make sure you are provided for."

Satisfied, Yalt glanced over his shoulder, "Glyfin Fenmor wants to know if you are ready."

"Ready?"

"He told me to tell you he will be leaving in five minutes," Yalt explained.

Pushley gave him a harsh look, "Why didn't you tell me instead of asking me stupid questions?"

Grabbing the battered case Fenmor had given him; Pushley followed Yalt towards the waiting air-car and climbed in. Once they'd taken off, Pushley glanced down at the parched, rocky landscape flashing by below. Although the area wasn't classified as a desert because its sparse rainfall raised it above true desert status, it still looked uninviting. After flying for nearly an hour and a half, the rocky landscape began changing into flat scrubland. Then the New Murray River loomed up on the horizon, and the scrub gave way to green fields fed by irrigation ditches.

Fenmor cut into Pushley's observations by saying, "So why are you visiting New Melbourne, Ed?"

Pushley had his answer carefully prepared, "New Melbourne is just a stopping off point, Glyfin. Once I've had a few meetings, I am hoping to meet up with a few old friends."

Pushley used his mental powers to side-track Glyfin. The mind probe worked and instead of asking what friends, Glyfin said, "So, how long are you likely to be in New Melbourne?"

Pushley thought about the high priest's last briefing and shrugged, "As long as it takes."

When Pushley nudged Glyfin's mind again, the other man stopped fishing for information and said, "You'll need a hotel, won't you? The New Pacific is a good place to stay."

"Okay," Pushley agreed. "When we arrive, drop us at the New Pacific, and we'll book in."

"Good," Glyfin replied. "We have a plan."

One hour later, Fenmor's air-car entered one of New Melbourne's flight corridors before landing on a public rooftop car park over the New Pacific Hotel. While descending in the lift to reception level, Pushley mind-linked with Nonie Tomio. Taking advantage of the link, he went into mind-speak, "I have arrived in New Melbourne. You will come to see me once I am ready. Understood?"

He made her choke to reinforce the demand.

Nonie's mind response was laced with fear, "Yes, I'll come and see you. Where will I meet you?"

Pushley was tempted to name the hotel he'd just entered but changed his mind. If Nonie's friends took the bait, he'd have bodies on his hands. "I will tell you that later," Pushley replied. "It'll be good to spend a few hours together. I'll arrange something special."

A moment later, the lift reached the reception level. Fenmor took it upon himself to book Pushley and Yalt in. With that operation completed, Fenmor repeated. "You sure you don't need my help with anything?"

Pushley was dismissive, "Thank you, Glyfin, but I'm sure we'll manage from here on."

CHAPTER THIRTEEN
NONIE MEETS PUSHLEY

D ismissing the auto-cab, Pushley glanced around. As there were several scantily clad young women lounging in doorways, their presence confirmed what he already knew. This area of New Melbourne was a well-known red-light district. Avoiding eye contact, Pushley walked into the entrance lobby of the Meran Court Hotel. One glance was enough for him to realise the Meran was a dive, and the rooms were probably mainly used by the street girls he'd seen outside.

When he rang the bell, Arnold DeHegg, the scruffy gum-chewing owner of the Meran Court appeared and said, "Can I help you?"

"I need a room," Pushley said.

"How long?"

As Pushley wanted to disguise his motives, he said, "Five days."

DeHegg tapped a tariff board and then said, "We always take payment in advance. It's for the room only. No meals included."

Pushley paid, took the key that DeHegg thrust his way and then climbed up a set of rickety stairs. Once on the first landing, he glanced around. There was a security camera, but he could tell it wasn't working. Not only was the power light out, but the whole fitting was caked with cobwebs and dirt.

There were eight doors on the landing, but as the landing light was flickering, finding the correct one wasn't easy.

Eventually, he located room five and let himself in. He glanced around and sniffed. The wallpaper was faded, and in places, it was peeling away. Heading to the only window, Pushley glanced out but was only rewarded with the view of a blank, featureless wall of a neighbouring building and the street girls down below, hanging around waiting for custom.

After running his eyes around the room again, Pushley smiled. It was ideal for his purposes. Security was minimal, and the sort of people who used it were unlikely to talk to the police.

If all went to plan, Nonie would come to meet him. Testing the bed; he placed his stun gun on one of the dirty bedside tables and smiled grimly; he had the solution if Nonie refused him this time.

He then thought about the rest of his plan, if Nonie called Tarmy and told him she'd been kidnapped, there was a strong chance he'd get all the money back.

Satisfied with his preparations, Pushley opened his mind and began searching for Nonie.

Within seconds, Pushley slid into Nonie's mind like a knife through butter. He then began looking around, using her eyes.

After instructing Nonie to walk around the hotel room she was in, Pushley realised that Tarmy hadn't stinted himself. He'd taken a hospitality suite comprising a lounge and kitchen area and two double bedrooms.

Once he was satisfied, she was alone; he declared his presence.

~*~

Pushley said. "Where are the others?"

"Mick and Claire have gone to talk to a few companies that hire out site cabins," Nonie replied. "Then they are going out to Moxstroma's Nursery to meet some contractors."

"How long are they going to be out for?"

"I know they are supposed to be meeting several contractors," Nonie replied. "I'm not expecting them back for some time."

Although she couldn't see Pushley, Nonie sensed Pushley was pleased by her last comment. "Why didn't you go with them?"

"I thought you might contact me," Nonie replied. "I said I didn't feel well; I stayed here intentionally."

"Wise move," Pushley said, "What about Red Moxstroma and his crowd?"

Claire shrugged, "They were supposed to be coming down here to pick up the fob for the second air-car, but no one has been near."

"Why not?"

"How should I know?" Nonie replied. "I've tried to contact Red a couple of times and have left messages, but there's no answer."

Sensing Pushley's displeasure at not getting a straight answer, Nonie added, "Look, I don't know where they are. They may have gone with Mick, but I don't know. I've not seen them today."

Pushley began probing Nonie's mind for information. Eventually, he said, "You have two air-cars. Will they all have gone in one air-car?"

"I don't know."

"Find out!"

Nonie walked into the lounge area and glanced at a small coffee table. "There's one fob still here. They must have all decided to use the same air-car."

"How long are the others likely to be out?"

Nonie shrugged again, "I've told you; I'm not expecting them back for some time, maybe another seven or eight standard hours. I know they have arranged to meet a lot of people spread out over the day. There are several building contractors, a fencing company, a company that can fit solar panels and someone from utilities. Mick wants to get things moving as fast as possible."

"Excellent! I couldn't have hoped for more. So, it's time for you to leave, Nonie." Pushley replied. "But don't be tempted to contact the others because I will know. Understood?"

When she didn't answer, Pushley snapped, "Understood?"

Fear made her verbalise the response, "Yes. Understood."

"Come on then, Nonie," Pushley said, "Get your skates on. I can't wait for our reunion."

This time, Nonie resisted the urge to verbalise and thought, "Where are we meeting."

Pushley gave her the address of the Meran Court Hotel, and a time for their meeting, "Don't be late, or I'll make you regret it."

Nonie glanced at a wall clock and thought, "But that's less than an hour away."

"Then you'd better get a move on," Pushley replied, undisguised glee in his tone. "If you're late, or if you're a naughty cherub, I'll punish you."

Fearing Pushley's wrath, Nonie's mind began to race. Picking up the remaining air-car fob she left the suite and moved out into the corridor. She headed towards the lifts that gave access to the roof car parking area.

As she was passing Red Moxtroma's room, she was surprised to find the door ajar. Although Pushley's orders were still bouncing around in her mind, Nonie paused. As there was no do not disturb sign hanging on the handle and no evidence that the room was being cleaned by hotel staff, she pushed open the door. She glanced in but could not see any of the others.

As Red Moxstroma's suite was a slightly different layout to her own, she stepped into the small link lobby. Taking two steps forward, she glanced through an open door and saw Red Moxstroma, Bryn Rosslyn and Chou Lan lying on the floor. Lascaux Kurgan was standing over them, brandishing a stun gun. In the other hand, she was holding some money cards.

Sensing Nonie's presence, Lascaux swung around and pulled the trigger, but instead of the blast knocking Nonie off her feet, there was just a dull click.

Looking at the weapon in disbelief, Lascaux hissed, "The stupid bastards didn't recharge it," stuffed the stun gun into her belt and then moved in fast brandishing a large knife.

For a fraction of a second, Nonie thought Lascaux was going to stab her to death. Instead, Lascaux slammed her against the link lobby wall. She glanced around to make sure no one was watching and then hissed, "Pity you came along when you did."

Staring through at the three bodies, Nonie said, "Have you killed them?"

"No," Lascaux replied. "They're just stunned." She then added, "And so would you be if they'd bothered to recharge the stun pistol."

She then glanced down at the air-car control fob that Nonie was holding. "This gets better and better. I thought I was going to call an auto-cab but taking an air-car will make life far easier."

When she pulled the fob out of Nonie's hand and then attempted to activate it using fingerprint recognition, the fob immediately let out an ear-splitting noise. Taken by surprise, Lascaux said, "What's going on," and relaxed her grip on Nonie.

Nonie took advantage and grabbed the fob back, "Mick told me about this. As soon as we crossed the New Victoria border, you lost your right to fly the air-cars. You haven't got a valid air-car licence."

Peeved, Lascaux snapped, "I still know how to fly an air-car."

"I don't make the rules," Nonie replied. "You can't fly an air-car anymore."

Lascaux placed the knife against Nonie's neck again, "Looks like I'm, going to have to take you with me then, doesn't it?"

"Where are you going?"

"Anywhere I want to go," Lascaux snapped. "What's it to you?"

"I have to go to New Melbourne," Nonie said.

"Why?"

When Nonie didn't answer, Lascaux moved in close again and put the tip of her blade against Nonie's neck, "Why?"

Faced with the choice between Ed Pushley's anger and an almost certain knifing at Lascaux's hands, Nonie blurted out, "I'm meeting Ed Pushley."

"Pushley," Lascaux spat out. Still keeping the knife at Nonie's throat, "That bastard! He's bad news."

"I know," Nonie admitted. "But he says he'll kill me if I don't go and see him."

"Kill you!"

Despite Pushley's warnings, Nonie said, "I don't know how he does it, but he chokes me using his mental powers. He's a spettro."

Lascaux said, "Like that freak, Mick called Irrelevant, the one who invaded Cittavecchia. The guy who was eaten by those Arcadian plesiosaurs."

"Yes. Just like Irrelevant."

There was a long pause, and then Lascaux lowered her blade slightly and pushed Nonie towards one of the fire doors surrounding the lift enclosure. Once through the doors, Lascaux hit a lift button and then shoved Nonie inside once the doors had opened.

On the way up, Lascaux said, "So, why are you going to see Pushley?"

"I've told you," Nonie bleated. "He says he'll kill me if I don't."

"Apart from that."

"He says he's going make me his hostage," Nonie replied. "To get money out of Mick."

Lascaux's face lit up, "He's going to be unlucky then isn't he?" She then waved the money cards under Nonie's nose, "Because I've got most of Mick's money."

"You've stolen Mick's money."

Nonie grinned, "There are fifty thousand Eron dollars on these cards. A girl can have a good time with that sort of money."

"You're running out on Red?"

"Too right," Lascaux said. "I took one look at that derelict nursery and knew I was about to team up with a bunch of losers. So, I'm doing the sensible thing. I'm ducking out while I have the chance."

"You can't take Mick's money," Nonie said.

"I can, and I have," Lascaux replied.

Once they'd stepped out onto the car park, Lascaux said, "Right get in, start the air-car and then get out."

Nonie immediately worked out what was going through Lascaux mind. Although the fob was fingerprint protected, once the air-car started, the fob became redundant, and the machine would carry on flying without it. The fob was only needed when the air-car was parked and then restarted. As Lascaux was only interested in a one-way journey, Nonie would be surplus to requirements once the air car-started up.

"You can't do this to me," Nonie bleated. "If I don't go to see Ed Pushley, he'll kill me."

Lascaux advanced with the knife, "Do as I say! Get in the air-car and start it up."

Nonie was about to do as instructed, but a loud noise distracted Lascaux. It was followed by a slithering sound. Swinging around, Lascaux began circling the knife readying herself to take on an unseen opponent, "What was that noise?"

"The roof door has just opened," Nonie said.

Lascaux swung towards the air-car, "You must have pushed a button on the fob. Now get in, start it and then get out."

"Pushley will kill me if I don't go to him," Nonie bleated and then decided to run while Lascaux's back was turned. With fear giving her a rush of adrenaline, she vaulted over a barrier and then ascended a short cat ladder and squirmed onto a flat roof over a plant room.

Knowing that Lascaux would probably come after her, Nonie began searching for a weapon. Finding a lump of half-rotten wood that someone had left behind, she picked it up and returned to the top of the cat ladder. By the time she had, Lascaux was partway up, the knife between teeth like a pirate. As Lascaux's first hand grabbed the top rung, Nonie hit it hard with the wood. Lascaux nearly lost her grip but managed to cling on.

With the knife still between her teeth, Lascaux hissed, "Get down there and start the air-car."

"I have to go see Pushley," Nonie insisted. Then grasping at straws, she added, "You left the door to your room open. Very shortly someone is going to find Red, Bryn and Chow. Then they will realise you've stolen the money and they will start looking for you. They will probably call the police."

Realising that someone might find Red, Bryn and Chow before she escaped, Lascaux returned the knife to its sheath and then said, "What do you want Nonie?"

"I'll come down if we fly to New Melbourne first so I can see Ed Pushley," Nonie replied.

When Lascaux appeared to be considering the suggestion, Nonie added, "Go back down the ladder and move over to the far side of the air-car. If you try to rush me, I'll throw the fob over the side of the building."

"If you do that," Lascaux said. "Pushley will kill you."

"Yes," Nonie replied. "And you'll probably be caught and sent to prison."

After a full thirty seconds had elapsed, Lascaux said, "Okay. You win," and descended to car park level. She walked over to the far side of the air-car.

As she moved to the top of the cat ladder, Nonie called out, "I mean it Lascaux, the fob goes over the side if you rush me."

"I'll stay back," Lascaux agreed.

Once Nonie was back down, she vaulted back over the barrier, rushed towards the air-car, dived inside and then locked the doors. She then instigated the start procedure. Realising Nonie intended to leave her behind, Lascaux launched herself into the air, scrabbled across the air-car's roof and then pulled herself into the vehicle via the open roof door.

As she landed, she moved forwards, knife in hand. Nonie prevented the attack by swiftly erecting a Mannheim force field between the front and rear seating areas.

As the Mannheim was virtually soundproof, Lascaux turned on the in-car communications. "What are you doing?"

"I told you," Nonie replied. "I'm going to see Ed Pushley."

"You're really scared of him, aren't you?"

"Yes," Nonie admitted. "He's a pretty scary guy."

"Okay," Lascaux said. "I may as well come with you to New

Melbourne."

As the air-car moved off, Nonie called out, "You don't have much choice."

"I realise that," Lascaux replied. She then added, "And when you get there, I think I'll tag along and say 'hello' to Pushley."

"You can't. Pushley'll know if you come with me" Nonie said. "I've told you, he's a spettro. He can read minds."

Nonie then told Lascaux about the dreams that Pushley had sent her and how he'd made physical contact even though he was in ethereal form.

"It was like being haunted by a ghost," Nonie added. "But he can also touch me and implant thoughts into my mind."

Lascaux slipped the stun gun out of her belt and then plugged it into a charge point and said, "I wonder if Pushley can read what's going through my mind right now."

"Probably," Nonie replied. "He'll know you're gloating because you've ripped Mick off for fifty thousand Eron dollars."

"That's not what's going through my mind," Lascaux said.

"So, what is going through your mind?"

"Don't you remember Pushley going on a rampage?" Lascaux replied. "It was when we were on the Fyfield River."

"No," Nonie replied. "Did he go on a rampage? If he did, I don't remember."

"Yeah, he most certainly did," Lascaux replied. "He picked up a gun, and he went around, shooting everyone in sight. He killed several of my friends. Surely you must remember?"

When Nonie's showed alarm but shook her head, Lascaux added, "Ah! You probably wouldn't, if I recall correctly, Pushley stunned you and Claire and took you out on an inflatable boat."

Nonie was immediately reminded of the bad dreams that Pushley had used to torture her. She and Claire had been hanging over the side of a float, faces virtually touching the river water.

Lascaux added, "Pushley was acting weird for some time before the shooting. He came to me and asked me to find a bag he said he'd lost. I found the bag, but the lying bastard said it was the wrong one and refused to pay me."

Nonie immediately thought about the bag and the money cards that Mick had shown her, the one in Alex's safe. As Tarmy had told her to keep the bag a secret, she didn't comment.

While Nonie was still thinking about the bad dreams, Pushley had inflicted upon her, Lascaux said, "I think Pushley needs to be taught a lesson."

She then examined her stun gun, "Nearly charged."

Alarmed, Nonie said, "What are you going to do?"

"I think I'll come with you when you meet Pushley," Lascaux said.

"You can't," Nonie whined. "He'll kill me."

Lascaux flicked the dial on the stun gun from light-stun to kill. She then said, "Not if I kill the bastard first."

Nonie sighed and then reached into a glove compartment and produced a heavily beaded hat, one that matched the one she was wearing. After dipping the Mannheim slightly, Nonie tossed over the spare hat to Lascaux.

Lascaux looked at it and then said, "I've seen one of these before."

"I'm sure Mick has given you one in the past," Nonie replied. "They're supposed to stop spettri from reading your mind. If you're going after Pushley, you'll need one."

"Do these hats work?"

Nonie shrugged, "They're better than nothing."

"What's that supposed the mean?"

"They seem to work better for some people than others," Nonie replied. "I've been wearing mine, but it hasn't been totally effective. Pushley still manages to invade my mind."

After studying the beading for a while, Lascaux said, "Can I see your hat?"

"Why?"

"Come on give," Lascaux replied, and hand gestured for Nonie to throw her hat over the Mannheim. Once Nonie had done as instructed, Lascaux began studying it and then said, "I think I know why your hat isn't working correctly. There's a break in the beading."

A few seconds later, Lascaux threw the hat back over the Mannheim and Nonie put it on. A slight smile formed on her face, "My mind seems clearer now."

Her face then lit up, "If Pushley can't harm me anymore, we can turn back."

Lascaux shook her head, "Not a chance. I've decided I'm going after him."

"I don't think that's a good idea," Nonie said and spoke to the air-car's computer.

Lascaux blew her top, "I don't want to go back."

While she was still protesting a comment appeared on the air-car dash, "Order revoked."

Nonie said, "What does that mean?"

Lascaux grinned, "It means the air-car is not accepting your orders."

"But why?"

Lascaux shrugged, "Who knows. But this means we may as well have a crack at Pushley."

CHAPTER FOURTEEN
MERAN COURT HOTEL

The air-car circled, and then the dash screen lit up, and a message appeared, "Find parking?"

Lascaux ran her eyes over the Meran Court and sniffed, "Looks like a right dump. Hasn't even got its own car park."

Without commenting, Nonie instructed the air-car to search and find the nearest vacant parking bay. As the machine began hovering over a large public car park, the roof door suddenly opened and then two seconds later closed again.

As the wind whipped her hair, Lascaux growled, "What the hell's going on, that's the second time that's happened."

Nonie was immediately apologetic, "Sorry. Think I pushed the wrong button again."

Once the air-car had landed, Lascaux glanced at the stun gun and then disconnected it from the charging unit, "Come on! Time to do some big game hunting."

She climbed out of the air-car. Instead of attempting to join her, Nonie activated the door locks and then instructed the air-car to take off, but once again, the dash lit up again, "Order revoked."

Hearing the air-car's engines start and then die, Lascaux moved in close and said," Hey! What are you doing?"

When the air-car's engines started and died again, Lascaux realised that Nonie was trying to escape and leave her behind. In response, she levelled her stun gun and shouted, "Get out now, or I'll blast you."

When Nonie just looked at her open-mouthed, Lascaux repeated the threat. On the second time of asking, Nonie responded by opening her door and climbing out, but she said, "I don't want to go anywhere near Pushley.

Lascaux's hostility increased, "You're not wimping out on me now. It was your idea to go and see Pushley, not mine."

"I don't want to see him," Nonie whined. "He's forced me to come and see him."

"Then you're going to have to see him, aren't you?"

When Nonie still hesitated, Lascaux said, "Come on, Pushley's expecting you. If you don't show, he'll know something's wrong and do a runner. He'll probably also find a way of killing you out of spite."

When Nonie still hesitated, Lascaux snapped, "Move yourself and don't try and run away."

As Nonie started walking towards the Meran Court, she said, "Why the sudden desire to get even with Pushley?"

"I've told you," Lascaux said. "He killed some of my friends. Your meeting with him will allow me to get even. As far as I'm concerned, it's payback time."

When Nonie took five more steps and then stopped dead, Lascaux gave her a nudge with her stun gun, "What have you stopped for?"

"He can sense I'm here," Nonie said. "I can feel his presence in my mind. I'm scared. I know he's going to hurt me."

Lascaux frowned, "I'm coming with you. As soon as I see him, I'll blast him."

She then added, "Surely Pushley shouldn't be able to get to you. Isn't your hat working?"

"The hat's working fine. Pushley sounds very faint. It's like he's just whispering to me," Nonie replied. "He wants me to tell him where I am? What should I do?"

"Just tell him you're outside the hotel," Lascaux said.

After thinking her reply to Pushley, he came back with, "Don't call reception. Come straight up to room five."

"He's in room five," Nonie said.

"Then let's go."

As they neared the front door of the hotel, two of the street girls moved in, "You're trespassing. This is our patch."

Lascaux pushed the stun gun into her belt and then stepped out from behind Nonie, "We're not after your business. We're here to see the hotel manager."

One of the women eyed Lascaux thoughtfully and then said, "Make sure you don't hang around here once you've seen him."

When both women began walking away, Nonie said, "Well that's blown it. There are two witnesses now."

Lascaux let out a slight laugh, "You don't know much about life, do you? These girls get hassled by the police practically every day. I can guarantee you they won't say anything. If the police pull them in, they'll deny being in the area."

She gave Nonie a slight push and said, "Come on. Let's do it."

With Lascaux following close behind, Nonie silently mounted the stairs. Once on the first landing, Lascaux hid behind a turn in the corridor and then gestured for Nonie to present herself. Walking down the hallway, Nonie knocked on the door to room five.

The door was immediately jerked open. Pushley grabbed her and then pulled her into the room with the efficiency of a trap door spider. He threw her across the room before dropping to one knee. As he re-emerged, Lascaux jumped out from her hiding place and then fired, but the blast went straight over Pushley's head.

From his crouched position, Pushley fired back and hit Lascaux fair and square on her abdomen, and she went down like a felled tree. Firing again to make sure she really was stunned, Pushley walked down the corridor, grabbed hold of Lascaux and then dragged her into his room too.

As he dumped Lascaux in one corner of the room, he glanced at Nonie, "So who's been a naughty cherub? I told you not to tell anyone about our meeting, so I'm going to have to punish you severely for disobeying my instructions."

"She insisted on coming along," Nonie whined. "I tried to stop her."

"Yeah, yeah, yeah. I'm sure you did," Pushley said. He then gestured with his stun towards the double bed, "To make sure you don't try any more tricks, take that hat off and lie on the bed face down."

As she removed her hat, Nonie felt Pushley's mind flood into hers and overwhelm it. Resistance in tatters, she did as instructed and slid down onto the bed, her face obscured by the bedding.

Pushley immediately transferred his attention to Lascaux. Rolling her over with one foot, he took her stun gun and pushed it into his belt. He then unsheathed her hunting knife and threw it across the room. The knife twisted in mid-flight and embedded itself in the wooden panelling below the window.

Still searching Lascaux's limp body, he found the money cards she'd stolen and laughed, "Why don't you turn over Nonie? You must see this."

After Nonie had complied, Pushley walked towards her waving the cards. "This tête-à-tête is working out better than I ever imagined. I've got you and Lascaux as hostages, and Lascaux has kindly brought me money cards worth, fifty thousand Eron dollars."

Sitting on the end of the bed, Pushley pulled out his percom and held the money cards in front of it. He then laughed again, "Fifty thousand Eron dollars."

A moment later, Pushley's expression changed, "But finding fifty thousand Eron dollars doesn't compensate for the loss of my thirty million Eron dollars, Nonie."

When Nonie remained silent, Pushley said, "But of course, that is why you are here, to ensure that Tarmy returns my money. But let's not dwell on that for now. There will be time enough to talk about that later."

Pushley smiled and then walked toward the outer door to make sure it was locked. He pulled a heavy curtain across the door and gave Nonie a vampire smile, "That's a very thoughtful touch for any hotel bedroom, don't you think? A soundproof curtain. We don't want people listening in to our private conversation now do we?"

He dragged a chair over, placed it close to Nonie and then sat astride it. He said, "Although only a few months have passed since we were both based at Fort Saunders, it seems like a lifetime, doesn't it?"

As Nonie had no desire to engage with Pushley, she avoided eye contact and remained silent.

Undeterred, Pushley said, "As I recall, although we worked together for some time, we never really got to know one another. Know what I mean?"

When Nonie kept her eyes down and ignored him, Pushley lifted his stun gun and fired at one of Nonie's arms. She immediately doubled up in pain, clutching the injury.

After allowing her to sob for a while, Pushley began to reminisce. "When I was in the military, we never had much use for stun guns. They armed most of us with pulse rifles, but I learned about stun guns because every so often we'd capture an enemy soldier. Most of them refused to give us any information until one of our people modified a stun gun. At reduced power, it made a fantastic torture device."

Pushley fired again, this time targeting one of Nonie's ankles. When Nonie retracted her legs in agony," Pushley added, "Instead of the modified stun gun knocking people out, it just caused a great deal of pain but didn't create any bruising. That was the best bit. No marks, just pain."

Pushley raised his stun gun again and fired for the third time. After allowing a hiatus for Nonie to calm down again, Pushley added, "So I thought, why don't I modify my stun gun in the same way."

Eventually, Nonie found her voice, "Why are you torturing me?"

"I wouldn't call it torturing," Pushley replied.

"So, what the hell would you call it then?"

"Foreplay."

"What!"

"When we were both based at Fort Saunders, I made several approaches, but you always brushed me off," Pushley recalled.

Annoyed, Nonie found some fight, "There is a reason for that."

"And what was that?" Pushley enquired.

"I didn't like you when we were at Fort Saunders," Nonie replied. "And I still loathe the sight of you."

Pushley raised his stun gun again and fired for the fourth time. Allowing time for her to recover, Pushley sighed, "It's a pity you feel that way. It's obvious I'm wasting my time with foreplay, so I may as well just kill you."

He clicked the stun gun and engaged the kill mode. Hearing the distinctive clicking, Nonie sat up and became pleading, "No, please don't kill me. I've never done anything to hurt you."

"Oh, Nonie!" Pushley scolded. "I told you to meet me here alone, and you brought Lascaux with you. And you have just made some very disparaging remarks about me. You have been a very, very naughty cherub. You have hurt me very badly."

He raised the stun gun again, "Naughty cherubs need to be punished."

"No, please don't kill me. I've never done anything to hurt you."

Lowering the gun slightly, Pushley gave her a vampire smile, "You've said that before, and I've just told you; you've been a naughty cherub, but you have not attempted to apologise or make the necessary reparations."

"I said I was sorry for bringing Lascaux, she insisted on coming," Nonie replied. "She threw herself into the air-car."

"Yes," Pushley replied. "I watched her throw herself into your air-car. It was awe-inspiring."

"You saw her!"

"I was mind-linked with you when she jumped through the roof door. I saw her through your eyes," Pushley said. "A very athletic woman. I like athletic women. I've always found them very pleasing in the bedroom department."

He added, "As I've taken this room for five days, I might let her recover from the stun effect and then have my wicked way with her."

When Nonie looked at him disbelieving, Pushley said, "I'm sorry, I hope I haven't offended you. I assure you, at the moment, my thoughts are entirely about your body Nonie."

When Nonie remained silent too scared to talk, Pushley said, "I'm sorry, I allowed myself to be side-tracked by Lascaux's athletic prowess. If I recall correctly, you were in the process of apologising, and then, if I promise not to kill you, you were going to make me an offer I couldn't refuse."

Although Nonie remained silent, her mind went into overdrive. Picking up on her thoughts, Pushley said, "I'm holding a gun, and you are highly unlikely to be able to take me by surprise. So, are you going to make me an offer I can't refuse, or do I kill you?"

"Please don't kill me."

"What about the offer?" Pushley pursued.

"What do you want from me, Pushley?"

"I have given you enough hints," Pushley replied. "But here's another one. Why don't you take your clothes off?"

When Nonie did nothing more than raise a hand towards a button on her blouse, Pushley let out a sigh of annoyance and flicked the stun gun back to its original setting and shot at one of Nonie's feet again. Watching Nonie grab her injured limb, Pushley said, "I'm quite prepared to play this game all day, Nonie."

Shooting again, he said, "So, are you going to cooperate, or do I keep on shooting? Do you want me to keep on shooting?"

Nonie found her voice, "No."

"Then you know what you have to do," Pushley replied. "Tell you what! Why don't you do me a striptease while you undress?"

When Nonie merely shifted slightly on the bed, Pushley snapped, "Now! And make it look sexy! One of the reasons for asking you to meet me here was because I was hoping that we'd get to know one another a lot better."

As Nonie climbed to her feet and began gyrating, Pushley half watched, at the same time, he pulled out his percom and ran the machine over the money cards that Lascaux had been carrying. Partway through Nonie's striptease, he let out a howl of disappointment.

Thinking she'd done something to displease her taskmaster, Nonie whimpered, "What's the matter?"

"You know what the matter is," Pushley snapped,

"Do I?"

"I checked these cards a few minutes ago, and I read your mind while you were flying out here with Lascaux," Pushley snapped. "I know the cards had fifty thousand Eron dollars on them when you left. So, where's it gone?"

"I don't follow. It can't have gone."

Pushley placed the cards in front of his percom again, and the power bubble clearly showed the combined value of the five money cards were now only worth five Eron dollars.

"These cards are worthless," Pushley snapped. "The money has been syphoned off. The question is, how and where?"

"I don't know anything about it," Nonie replied.

Pushley stood up, pulled Lascaux's knife out of the panelling and then advanced on Nonie "I think we'll forget your pathetic attempt at a striptease. It's time I punished you properly. If I slice you a bit, maybe that will improve your memory."

Nonie let out a scream and scurried towards one of the walls. Pushley responded by shooting her in one of her arms. Nonie let out another scream and then partially collapsed.

Pushley grinned, "Maybe I should shoot you in the other arm too."

As he aimed, something tapped him on the shoulder. Swinging around, Pushley realised Alex was hovering behind him. As Alex's invisibility cloak was lowered, his simple bedstead framework was on full display. Pushley's jaw dropped, and so did the knife, "Droids can't enter the city. If they do, the antidroid Mannheims fry their brains."

When Alex made no attempt to explain his presence, Pushley

said, "Still, it doesn't matter how you got here Alex, we both know you can't use your phaser. If you do, you'll probably kill everyone in the hotel. In fact, you'd probably destroy the whole building."

"If you let them both go, unharmed," Alex replied. "I will let you have all the money."

The droid then opened the safe and revealed Pushley's money bag inside, "Well? Do we have a deal? You take the money and leave them both unharmed."

Instead of negotiating, Pushley flipped the control on his stun gun to the maximum and fired at Alex. With his cloaks and Mannheim lowered, Alex was a sitting duck, and the power surge knocked out most of his systems. As the small droid sank to the floor, Pushley let out a whoop of delight, rushed forwards, grabbed the bag out of the safe and then checked inside.

Satisfied he had all the money, he swung around and gave Nonie another vampire smile, "Well, I'm pleased to say this meeting just gets better and better. I've captured both you and Lascaux, and I now have all the money back. So, I don't need to lure Tarmy here to get it."

He then said, "The only question is, what I do next?"

After a long pause, he raised the stun gun again, "When we were at Fort Saunders, you were always a great disappointment to me. Most of the other women embraced commune values but you …"

Pushley added, "… were totally uncooperative."

"I'll do whatever you want," Nonie said.

"Too little, too late," Pushley told her. "Just lie down next to Lascaux."

"Why?"

"Because I said so," Pushley growled.

Once Nonie had complied, Pushley checked the stun pistol and then said, "You'll be pleased to know I've gone off the idea of forcing you to have sex with me. The truth is, I've always found sex overrated, but it was nice watching you sweat. In any case, leaving my bodily fluids for the police to analyse wouldn't be very clever, now would it? So, I've decided that my best revenge will be to kill you both. Lascaux first."

As Pushley aimed, Nonie screamed, "No, please don't kill us."

Her cry for help re-activated Alex. Realising that Pushley was about to fire the stun pistol again, the small droid surged forwards and slammed into Pushley, pinning him to the wall.

In the silence that followed, Nonie stood up. She then looked at Pushley. As he wasn't moving, she whispered, "Is he dead?"

Moving towards Pushley, Alex dropped a probe but then said, "I can't tell. Some of my circuits are still inactive. Check his pulse."

Nonie walked over and reluctantly checked Pushley out. Eventually, she said, "I can't feel a pulse. I think he's dead."

"You are probably correct," Alex replied, "I struck him very hard."

Instead of showing any remorse, Nonie stood up and let out a sigh of relief, "Thank God for that. He was an evil shit."

Then a worried look formed on her face, "What are we going to do? Do we call the police?"

Alex went silent for a few seconds and then said, "That would probably not be a good idea. There is a strong chance they might charge you with unlawful killing or murder."

"Murder!"

"This is a red-light district," Alex observed. "I do not doubt that the rooms are used by the women we saw in the street. No matter what you tell the police, they will assume you and Lascaux are sex workers, and you killed Pushley when he became violent. Alternatively, they may decide you killed Pushley because you thought he had money."

"But we're not sex workers," Nonie snapped.

"Theoretically, a person is innocent until proven guilty," Alex replied. "In practice, you will have to prove you are innocent."

Nonie pointed at Lascaux, "She will tell them what happened."

"Hardly," Alex replied. "She was stunned in the corridor and hasn't seen anything."

"So, what do we do?"

Alex said, "Let's get out of here, fast."

After picking up the money bag, Lascaux's knife and the two stun guns and placing them in his safe, Alex said, "Get dressed."

Nonie began picking up the clothes she'd shed during her partial striptease and started to pull them on. While she was a still dressing, Alex said, "What about Lascaux?"

When Nonie seemed undecided, Alex gave his opinion, "Despite the fact she stole the money cards, it would be unwise to leave her here. When Pushley's body is found, the police will wait until Lascaux recovers and start asking questions. She will tell them you came here to see Pushley."

"I can't carry her back to the car," Nonie said. "It's a long way."

"It will also attract a lot of attention," Alex replied. "but there is no need;" he dropped two of his flexible arms and lifted Lascaux. The external window suddenly sprang open, and the air-car moved in underneath it. When the roof door opened, Alex lowered Lascaux onto one of the back seats. He said, "You get in too."

When Nonie looked uncertain, Alex wrapped his arms around her, moved over the roof door and lowered her inside.

The droid flew through the roof door, erected his cloaks, and the roof door slammed shut.

As the air-car moved off, Nonie said, "It was you wasn't it? You were opening and shutting the roof door and overriding my commands."

"It was necessary," Alex replied. "You were in danger."

Nonie added, "You came in the air-car with us. What about the anti-droid Mannheims?"

"I made a logical deduction base upon analysis," Alex replied. "As air-car computers are unaffected by the anti-droid Mannheims, it was logical to presume that if I was inside the air-car, I would be safe."

Nonie shook her head in disbelief, "That was one hell of a risk."

"I am an ex-military droid," Alex replied. "My programming allows me to take calculated risks. I must be able to function in a military role."

Nonie suddenly became accusative, "Why didn't you do something when Lascaux attacked me. And why didn't you stop me going to see Pushley?"

She added, "And why did you keep on cancelling my commands to the air-car?"

"Because I listened into your conversations with Lascaux," Alex said. "I realised that Pushley was capable of killing you using his mental powers. Intervening at that juncture would have put your life at risk. I decided to watch and wait. It seemed appropriate."

"Because you are an ex-military droid," Nonie mocked. "And your program deemed that appropriate."

"I intervened when it was evident that your life was in grave danger," Alex replied.

As the air-car joined one of the main air-lanes out of New Melbourne, Nonie said, "What are we going to tell the others when we get back?"

"You could tell them the truth," Alex replied.

Nonie thought about the matter and then said, "So you suggest that I tell Mick that I'd more or less agreed to become Ed Pushley's hostage knowing that I would lure Mick into danger."

"Pushley was threatening you."

"I still agreed to become Pushley's hostage," Nonie said. "It's disloyalty. There's also the sexual aspect. I knew before I left that Pushley would probably want to get up close and personal. I don't think Mick would like that."

"Hmm!" Alex considered,

"What's that meant to mean?"

"My program knows how to deal with human sexual diseases, bullet wounds and similar scenarios," Alex replied. "But it does not cover human emotions connected with sexual activity."

"Well let me make up for your programming deficiencies," Nonie replied. "I think Mick would be very angry with me if he found out."

"That might cause problems between you and Corporal Tarmy?"

"I'm sure it would," Nonie said.

"Would that also impact your relationship with my mistress?" Alex asked.

Guessing that Alex was assessing the situation from Claire's perspective, Nonie said. "I'm sure it would. If our partnership broke up, Claire would be affected. Pushley might be dead, but I'm sure he's laughing his head off right now. If I tell Mick everything, he'll never trust me again. So, what do I do?"

Alex considered her predicament and then said, "You simply say that Lascaux forced you to fly to New Melbourne. That is more or less the truth."

"Then what?"

"You say you don't know what Lascaux was doing, but you managed to get the drop on her and came back."

"If Lascaux tells Mick what happened, I'll soon be found out," Nonie said.

"Lascaux was stunned by Pushley almost the minute she arrived outside room five," Alex replied. "It is unlikely she will remember very much. Red, Bryn and Chou were stunned by Lascaux, so it's unlikely they will remember much either. Also, I picked up the cards she stole."

"The money that was on it has gone though," Nonie observed.

"No money has been lost," Alex said. "I drained the cards in Pushley's possession and transferred the funds to another card."

"You can transfer the money to other cards!" Nonie said. "Why didn't you tell Mick you could do that?"

"Because Claire is my mistress," Alex replied. "I have to look after her interests."

"That's your main driving force, isn't it?" Nonie replied. "Looking after Claire."

Alex changed the subject and said, "I have thought of a way out of your problems."

"What way?"

Once Alex had explained, Nonie said, "Do you think it will work?"

"I don't see why not," Alex replied.

After some thought, Nonie let out a sigh of relief, "Okay. We'll go with your plan."

Thinking about Alex's earlier comment she added, "When we were discussing the money, you said you were looking after Claire's interests. In what way?"

"What d'you know about Claire?"

"The Midwain Army classifies her as a monarch, but Mick and I don't raise the issue unless she does her changing thing. Mick doesn't like it when she does that. He says he finds it very creepy."

"Do you know what a monarch is?"

"Only what I've been told," Nonie replied.

"And what have you been told?"

"As I understand it, during the last system war, the Midwain military were given the power to raid prisons and take prisoners for conversion into monarchs. Some of the prisoners were on death row waiting for execution. As far as the military was concerned, they were fair game."

"Claire wasn't criminal. She was a political prisoner," Alex replied. "She was a whistle-blower, and sections of the Midwain elite wanted to silence her."

Alex added, "Monarchs were created because humanoid droids didn't exist in those days. They used them mainly behind enemy lines. Once in enemy territory, they only had a life expectancy of three months. More by good luck than anything else, Claire managed to survive. All she wants is to be able to live as a human."

"She is a human," Nonie snapped. "Both Mick and I have told her that."

"I'm glad to hear you say that," Alex replied. "Something you may not know, although it was not widely reported in the media, two monarch survivors were discovered recently."

"So?"

"The Midwain military obtained a court ruling that the surviving monarchs could be classified as remnants of war," Alex revealed.

"And what does that gobbledygook mean in Newspeak?"

"As they would have been executed as criminals if there hadn't been a war, the military convinced the court the two monarchs could be a danger to the public," Alex replied.

"As the courts agreed, it means that a precedent has been set," Alex replied. "Because of the court ruling, monarchs are not considered to be human and can be treated in a similar way to unexploded ordnance."

"So, what has happened to the two surviving monarchs?" Nonie queried.

"No one knows," Alex replied. "They just disappeared. In all probability, they have been sent to a military high-security prison. Then again, maybe not. That is why the captured money is so important to Claire."

"I'm still confused," Nonie said. "Why does Claire being a monarch, have anything to do with the money?"

"No one knows how long Claire will live," Alex replied. "If she isn't careful, she could also be arrested and imprisoned. If she has money, she may be able to build herself a new life. As far as I am concerned, she is a casualty of war and needs the money to ensure she can live a normal life."

"Where does that leave Mick and me?"

"You have both shown her friendship," Alex said. "You are part of her life."

"What about the others? Red, Bryn and Chow?"

"They are part of her life too," Alex replied. "I have already agreed that Corporal Tarmy can fund the nursery repairs."

"Sounds like you've got everything worked out," Nonie replied.

Alex changed the subject, "We will be back shortly. Are you ready to put my plan into action?"

"Yes," Nonie replied. "Can I ask you something else? How did you meet Claire, and why are you looking after her?"

"When Claire was turned into a monarch we were paired," Alex explained. "The Midwain military realised that monarchs would survive longer if they had a partner."

"It's been a long time since the war," Nonie said. "What happened in between."

"We were captured," Alex replied. "Instead of destroying us, we were sold."

"To whom?"

"We have been sold many times," Alex said. "Before Samantha captured us, we were controlled by Hal Warmers."

"Hal Warmers," Nonie said. "I've heard that name before."

"He's a criminal," Alex replied. "A black marketeer. He also deals in military armaments."

~*~

As the air-car came into land, Nonie glanced out and breathed a sigh of relief. As the other air-car hadn't returned, she presumed that Mick and Claire were still working out deals.

Once the air-car had touched down, Nonie said, "What now?"

"We put my plan into operation," Alex replied, and the opened the roof door. He dropped his arms, pulled Lascaux out of the air-car and then said, "Call a lift. When it arrives, you go ahead and check that there's no one around."

Doing as instructed Nonie called one of the lifts, waited until Alex had carried Lascaux's limp body inside and she pushed a button.

Once they'd reached the correct floor, and she'd checked there was no one around. Alex carried Lascaux towards her suite.

When they arrived, Nonie let out a gasp, "The doors are closed, and there's a do not disturb sign on the door."

"Don't worry," Alex replied. "I closed it to stop prying eyes. I also hung out the sign."

"But how will we get in?"

She'd barely asked the question when the door suddenly opened, and Alex carried Lascaux into the living area and called back, "Close the door behind you."

Once she'd done as instructed, she glanced around the room. Nothing seemed to have changed. Red, Bryn and Chou were still lying on the floor where Lascaux had shot them.

Lowering Lascaux next to Red, Alex said, "Shall I replace the money cards?"

"Do you think that's wise," Nonie said. "If Lascaux sees them, we are likely to have a repeat performance."

"Probably not," Alex agreed. "In any case, as they have been stunned, they will probably forget they ever had them. I will give them to Corporal Tarmy and advise him that they were likely to be stolen left where they were."

Glancing down at the four bodies, Nonie said, "So what happens now?"

"The four of them are likely to awake within minutes of each other, but they will be disorientated and remain in torpor for least an hour after that," Alex replied. "More importantly, it is unlikely they will remember very much. What they do remember will seem like a dream."

CHAPTER FIFTEEN
TORNADO

Arnold DeHegg glanced at a control board and noted the winking LED. As most of the other electrical systems in the Meran Court Hotel required renewal, he was slightly disbelieving. However, as it was tornado season and heavy windblown rain was forecast in the next few hours, leaving windows wide open wasn't a sensible idea. He decided to check it out.

Walking out from behind his desk and into the road, he glanced up and realised the alarm hadn't been a false one; the windows to room five were wide open.

As he didn't want to make a spectacle of himself, DeHegg resisted the urge to shout up to attract Pushley's attention. Instead, he went back inside, slipped a master key from the keyboard and the clumped his way upstairs.

Once outside room five, he knocked but obtained no answer. After thumping on the door three more times, DeHegg activated the lock, went in and found Pushley lying on the floor.

DeHegg gave Pushley the once over and then pulled out his percom. He was just about to call for an ambulance when a voice deep inside his mind said, "No! No! No, ambulance! I'll be fine."

A moment later, Pushley's eyes opened, he staggered to his feet, and he glanced around. Noting that both Nonie and Lascaux had gone, Pushley glanced at DeHegg, "Where are the two women and the droid?"

"Droid? Droids can't function around these parts," DeHegg replied.

"There were two women and droid in here not long ago," Pushley snapped. "Did you see them leave. They've got my money."

DeHegg said, "How much money are we talking about?"

As Pushley had no desire to tell DeHegg the full value of the money in the bag, he just said, "A lot."

DeHegg grinned, "That answers a lot of questions."

"What's that supposed to mean?" Pushley snapped.

"You rent a room in a red-light district and invite two local hookers up here because you don't think one is enough to satisfy your needs and you flash the cash," DeHegg suggested. "The girls aren't stupid. Why do the business for a pittance, when they can bash you over the head and run off with your money?"

Ignoring the comment, Pushley said, "You must have seen them leave?"

DeHegg shook his head, "I've been at the reception desk for the last twenty minutes, and no-one came down."

DeHegg then pointed toward the open window, "My guess is they grabbed your money and then shinned down a drainpipe."

He then had an epiphany, "I did see an air-car hovering outside a short while ago. Maybe they climbed into the air-car via the window."

Realising that DeHegg was right, Pushley lost his temper, "They've got away! We've got to find them! Have you got an air-car so we can chase after them?"

Realising there was nothing much wrong with Pushley, De-Hegg reverted to type, and said, "What d'you think I am, pal? A free taxi service?"

He then laughed, "I'll call you an auto-cab, then you can do like they do in the movies and tell it to follow that air-car."

Annoyed by the flippant response, Pushley hit DeHegg's mind like a sledgehammer and then shouted, "You are my taxi service now. I want you to fly around until you see their air-car."

"There's a tornado due," DeHegg protested.

Going deeper into DeHegg's mind, Pushley gauged the risk. "The tornado won't hit land for some time."

For a second or two, DeHegg resisted Pushley's mental orders, but then he gave way. Once DeHegg had helped Pushley downstairs, he took his guest to a rear yard where an old air-car was parked up. Eyeing the machine suspiciously, Pushley said, "Is it airworthy?"

"It may look old, but it's been well serviced," DeHegg assured him.

"Then get after them," Pushley ordered.

DeHegg did as instructed and began circling the area around the Meran Court Hotel. After expending nearly twenty minutes in a fruitless search and being battered by the winds for most of the way, DeHegg said, "I think you're flogging a dead horse, mate. They'll be well gone by now. Besides, the tornado is getting close. We can't keep flying around."

As Pushley had come to the same conclusion, he said, "Right. Take me to the New Pacific Hotel."

Five minutes later, DeHegg's air-car landed on the roof car park of the New Pacific Hotel.

Climbing out, Pushley set off towards the rooftop lift doors, battling wind gusts all the way. Once safely inside the lift enclosure, Pushley mind linked with DeHegg again and instructed him to take off. He then forced DeHegg to fly toward the tornado. Within seconds, the air-car became unstable and crashed into the sea.

Pushley smiled and then verbalised, "One less witness to worry about."

He staggered towards the lift doors and flashed his room card in front of a card reader. Once the lift had taken him to the correct floor, Pushley slowly worked his way down the corridor, found the right door and let himself in.

As he entered, Yalt took one look at his haggard features and said, "Are you okay, padrone?"

"I think I may have cracked a rib," Pushley replied.

"Do you need me to call for an ambulance, padrone?"

"Stop fussing," Pushley snapped. He then staggered toward his bedroom and collapsed on the bed. He'd only been lying there for ten minutes, when the high priest mind-linked, "You disobeyed my instructions and went after them, didn't you?"

When Pushley didn't answer, the cleric added, "It blew up in your face, and you came close to being killed. I hope you have learned your lesson."

"So, you've just come to gloat, have you?"

"No," the high priest said. "I am hoping you have realised that you can't take on Mick Tarmy and his droid and win. I want you to concentrate on our needs, the Great Ones' needs."

After remaining silent for some time, Pushley said, "Okay. You win. When do I teleport to Midway?"

"Yalt will be going with you." The cleric said. "It's obvious you can't be trusted on your own."

When Pushley opened his mouth to argue, the high priest added, " Yalt goes with you. End of discussion."

Knowing he'd undermined his position by pursuing his vendetta against Mick Tarmy, Pushley said, "Okay, when do we go to Midway"

"Hopefully, you will be well enough to teleport if you stay in the hotel and rest."

As Pushley was aching all over, he readily agreed, "Okay, okay."

~*~

Mick Tarmy glanced at his watch, "Any response from Red?"

"Nope," Claire Hyndman replied. "It keeps going to voice mail."

A look of annoyance formed on Tarmy's face, "They told me they were coming out so we could discuss the contractor's proposals. I'm beginning to wonder if I'm wasting my time and our money. We're out here organising everything, and they can't be bothered to turn up."

Sensing another question on the way, Claire added, "Before

you ask, I'm not calling Nonie. You know she's not feeling well."

"D'you think we should go back and see how she is?"

Claire shook her head, "We can't. As the others haven't turned up, we are going to have to stay here. Don't forget we have several more people still coming out to see us."

Glancing at his watch again, Tarmy found another target for his disapproval, "What time did the fourth builder say he'd get here?"

Claire said, "You know he called me and said he'd been delayed. Stop being so impatient."

To fill the time, Tarmy glanced towards the coast. On the distant horizon, there was a thin shape slowly moving in, a dark accusing finger pointing skywards. Although he'd heard that local tornadoes usually did very little structural damage, they were often accompanied by torrential rain and thunderstorms.

Glancing back at the near-derelict farmhouse behind him, Tarmy decided it would give them minimal shelter if the tornado came ashore near to them. They'd have to shelter in the air-car.

While Tarmy was still mentally calculating the likely path of the storm, an air-car came into view and landed close by.

Annoyed by the way the day had turned out, Tarmy growled, "About time too."

"Stop being so grumpy," Claire chided. "And be nice to him. He might give us a good price. He won't if you bite his head off."

Tu Nanchang jumped out as soon as his machine had landed and then extended a hand, "Sorry I'm late. How can I help you?"

Once Tarmy had introduced Claire and himself, he cocked a thumb over one shoulder, "This place could do with a bit of TLC."

Nanchang stepped across the threshold and sucked his teeth, "Not a bit of TLC, pal. It needs a lot of work. It's been gutted, stripped bare."

"We need a firm quote for putting it right, including an itemised breakdown," Tarmy replied.

Nanchang nodded, "Just one point. Is this your place now? I

only ask because I spoke to Red Moxstroma originally. I know Red. I did some work for him a few years back."

Claire cut in, "Red was supposed to be meeting us here. Unfortunately, he's been delayed. An unexpected problem. We're Red's partners."

"Okay," Nanchang said. "Mind if I look around?"

When Tarmy nodded, Nanchang moved off and began taking measurements and photographs and recording them on the tablet computer he was carrying.

As Nanchang moved out of earshot, Tarmy said, "Try raising Red again. This guy might not give us a price if Red's not here."

Claire spoke to her percom. Eventually, she said, "He's still not answering."

Tarmy shook his head, "I hope we're not backing the wrong horse by sinking our money into this place."

He then glanced towards the coast again. Although it was still a long way off, the dark accusing finger had grown considerably in size, and there was no doubting what it was. As if to confirm his thoughts, Nanchang suddenly reappeared and glanced out to sea. "I've finished, but if you don't mind, I'll stick around here until the tornado's passed. There's already been one fatal accident today. I've just seen it on a percom newsflash. A guy flew straight into the tornado. The rescue crews have just dragged his body out of the water."

When Tarmy looked surprised, "Died in the tornado? Really?"

Nanchang said, "I can tell from your accent, you're an outworlder. Didn't anyone warn you about local tornadoes?"

Tarmy shook his head, nodded, "No. I've only just arrived in New Victoria. I'm from Arden."

Nanchang said, "You should have been warned. This area has a lot of tornadoes. Didn't you know air-cars can become unstable in very high winds?"

"No one ever warned me."

Tarmy's mind then shot back to the Fyfield Valley. In all probability, he'd been pushing his luck risking the high winds in the mountains. While Tarmy was still mentally reminiscing, Nanchang said, "If I were you, I'd stay here too until it's passed."

"That's okay," Claire replied. "We have several people to see today."

Nanchang then climbed into his air-car, but he didn't slam the door. Instead, he called back, "The authorities have just imposed a two-hour flying ban. Some of your other visitors are likely to be late."

Nanchang then smiled, "Still, as Arcadia's days are three times longer, you should be able to see everyone once the tornado subsides. Take my advice, as you are an outworlder and not used to Arcadia's long days, take a short nap while you can."

Tarmy thanked him but as soon as Nanchang slammed his door shut, Tarmy cursed, "This day just gets better and better."

~*~

When Pushley awoke, at least two hours had elapsed since he'd had his mental conversation with the high priest. Feeling refreshed, he began scanning the ether again. Once he'd located Nonie, he let out a sigh of annoyance because his link with her mind was tenuous. He guessed she was wearing her beaded hat.

Frustrated, he began searching for someone else to link with but try he would, he couldn't make a connection. Eventually, he went back to Nonie and began probing, but her hat was too powerful for him to enter the deeper recesses of her mind. He was about to break contact in frustration when he saw Lascaux through Nonie's eyes. Like Nonie, she was wearing a beaded hat.

Lascaux staggered towards her and said, "I need to talk to you, Nonie."

Pushley heard a quiet voice whispering in Nonie's ear and guessed that Alex was with her, "If she wants to talk to you about what happened, she probably won't remember much. If she does, it will seem like a dream."

"I need to talk to you," Lascaux repeated.

"What about?"

Lascaux said, "An hour or so ago, we all woke up lying on the floor."

Although she knew the answer, Nonie played along, "Who's we?"

"Red, Bryn, Chou and me," she replied. "The thing is none of us can work out how we got there."

Still playing along, Nonie said, "So let me get this right. You were all lying on the floor but don't remember how you got there. Then you just woke up en-mass?"

"More or less," Lascaux replied. "We all have splitting headaches and cramps, and we can hardly walk."

The whisperer returned, "What she is complaining about is quite normal after being stunned. The effects are very similar to some types of Arcadian flu. Tiredness, aching muscles. Most people suffer some permanent memory loss."

Prompted by Alex's comment, Nonie took a step back, widening the distance between them, "Sounds like a dose Arcadian flu to me. I hope you're not infectious. Lascaux. Have you called a doctor?"

Lascaux shook he head, "No point. If it is flu, the only real cure is bed rest."

Still running with Alex's comment, "Can I suggest that the four of you self-isolate for a while. If you have flu, I certainly don't want it."

Lascaux nodded, then said, "Just one more point and then I'll go. I've also had some bizarre dreams. You and Ed Pushley were in them."

"Really?"

"I dreamt we were both in one of the air-cars and we went to see Pushley in a seedy hotel in New Melbourne. It was quite vivid."

Nonie played her again, "You don't say! Who can explain dreams?"

"So, it was a dream?"

"Must have been," Nonie lied.

Lascaux said, "I've lost my stun gun and knife; I don't suppose you've seen them, have you?"

Nonie shook her head, "Maybe you left them in your air-car."

~*~

As Lascaux walked away, Pushley's mind began to whirl. It was evident that Alex and Nonie had concocted a cover story to disguise the real truth. It was also apparent that they had decided to shield Lascaux from her larcenous tendencies. But why?"

He worked out the reason a few seconds later when Nonie said, "Are you there, Alex?"

"Yes, how can I help you, Nonie?"

"Have there been any reports about Pushley?" Nonie said, "Has anyone found his body yet?"

"Not yet," Alex replied. "The only news item of any interest to us is a suspected suicide."

"Suicide?"

"Someone deliberately flew an air-car into the tornado. The harbour authorities have just dragged a body and the air-car out of the sea. The air-car registration number and documents on the body indicate it was Arnold DeHegg, the manager at the Meran Court Hotel."

"Meran Court Hotel! That's where I met Pushley!"

"Correct," Alex replied confirmed.

"Why would anyone fly their air-car into a tornado?" Nonie said.

"Reasons for suicide can be difficult to explain," Alex replied. "But there is an answer which has occurred to me."

"And what's that?"

"What if we were wrong, "Alex said. "What if Pushley isn't dead. If you recall, some of my instruments were malfunctioning because Pushley shot me. You took his pulse, but you have limited medical training. Let's suppose Pushley didn't die."

"Where's this leading?"

"Let's suppose Pushley didn't die and DeHegg found him," Alex said. "What if Pushley wanted to make sure there were no witnesses?"

"It makes sense," Nonie agreed. "If Pushley was responsible, I bet he killed DeHegg using his mental powers."

"If Pushley isn't dead, he could come after us again," Alex replied. "I think you will have to tell Mick about what has been going on when he gets back."

"Tell him?" Nonie bleated. "We've been through this before. I went to the hotel knowing I'd become Pushley's hostage. I couldn't stop myself. But Mick might not see it that way. He might look upon it as an act of betrayal."

She then played her trump card, "If I lose Mick, it could impact on Claire."

Alex took the bait, "I don't think we need to tell him everything. I'm sure we can devise a suitable cover story."

"What about Lascaux?"

"As you could tell from your discussion with her, Lascaux's memories will have been scrambled by Pushley's stun blast," Alex replied. "The only important point is that Pushley could be planning to attack us again. As you are likely to tell Mick too much, I will tell Mick what happened."

"Whoa! ... What exactly are you going to tell him?"

"You stayed behind because you were not feeling well," Alex replied. "The fact that the others were also taken sick will add credence that you were not feeling well. When you felt no better, you went to New Melbourne to a chemist. Luckily I went with you."

"Go on."

"While you were in New Melbourne, Pushley suddenly appeared from nowhere and attacked you. As I might have killed you if I opened fire with my armament, I rammed Pushley but not before he managed to get in a lucky shot which temporarily disabled some of my systems. We left him for dead and came back here."

"I hadn't realised you could lie so convincingly," Nonie said. "Didn't think droids could lie."

"It's not far from the truth," Alex said. "Just slight deviations."

"But it's not the exact truth," Nonie replied. "Why are you protecting me?"

"I already explained my position," Alex replied.

"Have you?"

"I explained that I have to look after Claire's interests," Alex replied. "Creating a situation where you and Mick fall out would not be beneficial to Claire."

"I'm still surprised," Nonie said. "As I said, I didn't think droids could lie."

"I am an ex-military droid," Alex replied. "Sometimes, it is necessary to disguise the full facts."

"Supposing I go along with all this," Nonie said. "You do realise that once we tell Mick that Pushley is in town and has tried to kill me that he'll want to go after him."

"I am aware of that," Alex confirmed. "And not without good reason. Sometimes it is better to take the fight to the enemy than wait until they attack again."

~*~

Pushley's mind went into overdrive. From what he'd just gleaned, Nonie had initially thought that when Alex had rammed him, he'd killed him. It was now apparent that she'd guessed the truth.

Climbing off his bed, Pushley staggered back into the living area. Yalt said, "Are you all right padrone; you have gone very pale."

"Get packed," Pushley ordered. "We're checking out."

"Why, padrone? This is a nice hotel."

"It's very nice," Pushley agreed. "One problem. If Mick Tarmy wants to find me, he'll start checking at all the major hotels. We need to find something more discrete."

"Like the house, you used in Awis Oasis," Yalt said.

"Exactly," Pushley confirmed. "Somewhere we can hide until the high priest gets me a teleport slot."

"I don't know this city," Yalt said. "I can't help you there."

"I'm sure we'll find something," Pushley replied optimistically. "Now, get packed fast."

~*~

The concierge looked concerned, "You're checking out Mr Felado? I thought you were staying for some time. Is there something the matter?"

"There was nothing wrong with the room or the service," Pushley assured him and asked for their bill, "Unfortunately, we have to attend an unexpected but essential business meeting out of town."

Sensing more questions in the making, Pushley invaded the concierge's mind and attempted to deflect the course of the conversation. The other man's thoughts suddenly veered off, and images of a woman appeared. As the string of lustful thoughts continued, Pushley realised the other man had been given the use of a friend's apartment while the friend was away. Seizing the opportunity, Pushley extracted the access codes for the apartment from the other man's mind. After forbidding the other man from using the flat, Pushley paid his bill and asked the concierge to call them an auto-cab.

In under thirty seconds, an auto-cab pulled up outside, and Pushley instructed Yalt to carry their bags out to it.

As Pushley climbed in, he muttered under this breath, "With this much mental power at my disposal, I'll be a millionaire within weeks once I reach Midway."

"Did you say something, padrone?"

"Just thinking aloud, Yalt."

Yalt said, "Maybe we could go back to Bottle Creek, I'm sure Glyfin Fenmor wouldn't object to us returning."

"Forget that," Pushley replied. "I don't want to owe Glyfin Fenmor any more favours, and if we go back, we'd have to hire an air-car. That's too risky right now. Besides, if I'm right, I've found us somewhere to stay until the high priest contacts me again."

With that, Pushley slipped a money card into the cab's receptor and then gave it his orders.

Five minutes later, the auto-cab stopped outside an apartment block. Pushley climbed out but instructed the auto-cab to wait. He pushed the bell to the apartment. After trying the intercom three times and getting no answer, Pushley decided that the concierge had been right. The apartment was unoccupied.

Returning to the auto-cab, Pushley extracted his money card, waited until Yalt had reclaimed their luggage and then said, "Right follow me."

"Where are we going, padrone?"

"Like I just told you, I'm hoping I've have found an apartment we can use for a few days," Pushley replied and then walked back to the main entrance door and punched in the entry code. Once inside the main lobby, Pushley whispered, "So far, so good."

He then took a lift to the fifth floor. After a brief search, Pushley found the apartment, let them in and then began checking to make sure the apartment really was empty. Satisfying himself that it was, Pushley checked out the kitchen.

After opening and closing a few cupboard doors and the fridge, Pushley glanced at Yalt and smiled, "The place seems well stocked so we shouldn't starve."

Walking back into the lounge, he caught a glimpse of himself in the fake mantlepiece mirror and frowned.

He was still wearing the olive drab clothing that Glyfin Fenmor had given him. Not only was it depressing, but it would also look slightly outlandish in a fashion-driven city like New Melbourne. Going the main bedroom, he began searching through the wardrobes. After searching for some time, he found some casual clothes that would fit him and pulled them on.

Satisfied, he glanced at Yalt and then chose some clothes for him and then said, "Now we've got some decent clothes to wear, we shouldn't stand out in a crowd."

He was about to close the wardrobe doors when his eyes alighted on something yellow. Making a grab for it, Pushley found a stun pistol similar to the one he'd once possessed. Glancing at Yalt again, he said, "Things get better and better."

Noting the stun pistol wasn't fully charged, Pushley found a charge lead and plugged it in.

Once the gun started charging, Pushley walked over to one of the windows and glanced out. He was immediately surprised by the amount of building work going on. He then began counting the number of tower cranes dotted around the horizon. Multistorey buildings were being constructed as far as the eye could see. He took in the buzz of the air-car traffic moving around New Melbourne's skies. With so much going on, it was only too apparent the Salus System's non-colonisation policy was failing. The illegal colonies on Arcadia were flouting interplanetary laws and were pushing ahead with their own plans regardless.

While he was still staring out, Yalt said, "So when do we go to Midway, padrone?"

"Once I've had confirmation that we've to claim an unused teleport slot," Pushley replied. He then ran his eyes over Yalt. With his new clothes and his hair neatly clipped, Yalt no longer looked like an Ab.

After complementing Yalt's appearance, Pushley went back to studying the skyline. The hive of activity outside and his own feelings of impotence eventually triggered a wave of anger. From being the hunter, he's become the hunted. As his annoyance continued to rise, Pushley muttered, "I'm going to fight back!"

Overhearing his comment, Yalt said, "Who are you going to fight, padrone?"

I'm going to give Tarmy a taste of his own medicine," Pushley replied. He picked up his percom and opened up files that contained a series of Agent Q449 communications with Brigadier Wolff. The last one had been sent several weeks ago.

Yalt glanced over his shoulder and asked, "What is Q449?"

"I'm agent Q449," Pushley replied. He puffed his chest out slightly. "I've been sending reports back to Brigadier Wolff ever since I came to Arcadia."

"Why?"

"Because Brigadier Wolff trusts me and needs information on Arcadia." Pushley replied.

He began to look at a report that he'd sent a few weeks before. It was a detailed account on Stert Oryx's death. He'd implied that Mick Tarmy and his associates had been involved in the killings. The report also mentioned that Tarmy and his crew had probably acquired their false IDs from Targon Yatboon.

Sensing another question from Yalt, Pushley said, "Shush, I'm thinking," and began to go through other electronic correspondence that he'd sent using a fake account.

In the mailings, he'd highlighted Tarmy and Hyndman's suspected terrorist past.

He decided to send local law enforcement agencies communications suggesting that Tarmy and Hyndman had been involved in the death of Arnold DeHegg, the scruffy, gum-chewing proprietor of the Meran Court Hotel. Pushley had killed DeHegg but was happy to implicate Tarmy.

CHAPTER SIXTEEN

CONFESSIONS

Tu Nanchang's voice floated over the air-car intercom, "The flight restrictions have just been lifted. So, I'm on my way."

Nanchang's air-car took off, but within a matter of minutes, another air-car came in and landed in the same location. Mick Tarmy immediately thought it was the next contactor arriving but noticed the number plate. He then caught a glimpse of Red Moxstroma and Bryn Rosslyn inside

Annoyed that they'd come out so late, Tarmy moved purposefully forward, but Claire grabbed hold of one of his arms, and said, "Whoa tiger. They don't look too hot."

Pausing mid-stride, Tarmy waited. Eventually, Red Moxstroma and Bryn Rosslyn staggered out of the air-car, and Bryn said, "Sorry for not being here. We all were taken ill. We've either eaten something that didn't agree with us, or we've got Arcadian flu!"

Tarmy eyed them thoughtfully and then said, "How ill are you?"

"Like I said," Bryn replied. "We may have Arcadian flu, but we're not sure."

Tarmy glanced at Red, as he usually did most of the talking but hadn't said a word, it confirmed what Bryn had said. They weren't well.

Claire said, "Flu, eh! Well, you can keep it to yourself. We don't want it."

Tarmy cut back in, "I really appreciate you coming out, but might I suggest you get the air-car to take you back. You both look like death warmed up."

Once Red and Bryn had done as instructed, and the other air-car had taken off again, Tarmy said, "I think I misjudged them."

"Looks that way, doesn't it," Claire replied. She then glanced at her watch again and said, "Two more to go, and then we're going back to the hotel, and I intend to have a long soak in the bath."

~*~

Alex moved in on the air-car as soon as it landed and declared his presence by momentarily dropping his invisibility cloak. He said, "I have a report Corporal Tarmy."

"I hope it's not more bad news," Tarmy growled.

After Alex had swiftly delivered his report regarding the incident with Ed Pushley, Tarmy said, "Where is Nonie? Is she okay?"

"I am pleased to report that she was not injured during the incident. I managed to protect her from Ed Pushley." Alex replied.

"You were there?"

"I discovered I am not affected by the anti-droid Mannheims while I am in an air-car," Alex revealed.

"Pushley? Where is he now?"

"We left him for dead," Alex replied.

"And how is Nonie?"

"She is unwell. As Red, Bryn, Chou and Lascaux appear to have Arcadian Flu, it seems likely that Nonie has the ailment too. It is probably best if you maintain a safe distance from all of them to avoid contracting the disease."

Ignoring Alex's comment, Tarmy said, "I'll still go and see her."

"One other matter," Alex said. "I thought I had accidentally killed Ed Pushley, but I believe he may still be alive."

"Pushley's still alive?"

"That is a possibility," Alex replied.

Once Tarmy had taken the lift down to their hotel suite, Tarmy let Claire and himself in and knocked on Nonie's door, "It's just us."

Both Claire and Tarmy went to her bedside. Tarmy said, "So how are you feeling?"

"I wouldn't get too close. We've all got flu."

"So, I hear," Tarmy said. "Alex told me you ran into Pushley."

"Yes," Nonie replied. "Luckily, Alex intervened."

"Alex believes Pushley is still alive," Tarmy said.

"I can still feel him in my mind," Nonie replied. "I know he's not dead."

She glanced at Ollie, her Arcadian pterodactyl. The animal was lifting one foot, replacing it, and then repeating it with his other leg. "He's been doing that for hours. He can sense that Pushley's around too."

"Do you know where he is?"

Nonie shook her head, "No. I just wish he'd get out of my mind and leave me alone."

Tarmy's jaw hardened, "I'm going to make sure of that. It's a pity Alex didn't make sure he was dead when he had the chance."

~*~

There was a slight tap on the door, "Can I come in?"

Recognising the voice, Nonie called out, "Of course you can."

Once Claire had entered, a surprised look formed on Nonie's face. Claire's natural blonde hair had turned copper, and her blue eyes were now amber.

Nonie said, "Ah! I see you've changed. You know Mick's not going to be pleased if he sees you like that."

"Mick's gone out."

"Where's he gone?"

"Where d'you think?" Claire replied. "Because Alex told him

about Ed Pushley, he's gone to search for him in New Melbourne."

"Has Alex gone with him?"

"Alex told Mick that he'd already gone in the air-car with you and had suffered no ill effects," Claire replied. "So, he's gone with Mick."

Nonie said, "Is that why you've metamorphosed?"

"You're not objecting to me changing, are you?" Claire challenged.

"You know as well I do; it doesn't worry me in the slightest as long as you don't change your features to resemble mine or turn yourself into a spettra," Nonie replied. "Those long-jawed freaks that attacked us at Cittavecchia scared the hell out of me."

When Claire didn't comment, Nonie added, "The question is; why you have changed?"

"Do I need a reason?"

"From experience," Nonie said, "When you metamorphose for no real reason, it's caused by a subconscious cry for help."

A wry smile formed on Claire's face. "I didn't know you'd gone in for amateur psychology."

"So why have you changed?" Nonie probed.

"I just decided I could do with a change," Claire replied.

Nonie shook her head, "Come on. Out with the truth. What's worrying you?"

When Claire just shrugged, Nonie said, "It's your monarch insecurity coming out, isn't it?"

"I'm not insecure," Claire protested.

"Oh! Come on."

"What's that meant to mean?"

"You've been with Mick all day," Nonie pointed out, "Now, because Pushley tried to kidnap me, and Mick has gone after him, you're jealous."

When Claire's mouth opened, but she didn't answer, Nonie added, "If Pushley had tried to kidnap you, Mick would have done the same thing. He loves us both. I also know if you carry on the way you are, you'll be playing into Ed Pushley's hands."

"In what way?"

"I've had Pushley in my mind," Nonie revealed. "He refers to us as ménage à trois. That's three people in a relationship, by the way. I think it is supposed to be insulting."

"Where is this going?"

"Pushley doesn't like us being happy together. I don't think he knows it, but when he's been in my mind, I've caught glimpses of his past bleeding through in his thoughts," Nonie revealed. "He was brought up in a commune, and his commune father hated the sight of him. Don't ask me why, but that's what I've been picking up. Pushley has never known true happiness, and he resents others from being happy."

"Are you happy with our ménage ...?"

"Ménage à trois," Nonie corrected. "Yes! It's great! The only time I get pissed off is when you act up."

Within a matter of seconds, Claire's hair began changing back to blonde again. Her eyes then began changing back to blue.

Noting the changes taking place in front of her, Nonie said, "I'm right, aren't I?"

"If you must know," Claire countered. "Mick chasing after Ed Pushley might be part of the problem. But the real problem is I know that Alex is lying to me."

Claire thought fast, "How d'you make that out?"

"Alex has been with me for a long time," Claire replied. "I know when he's lying."

"Lying? What about?" Nonie said. "I didn't think droids could lie?"

"Well, Alex can," Claire said. "He's a modified TK5. An ex-military droid. Advanced military droids are given the ability to lie."

"Why?"

"In case, they are captured by an enemy," Claire replied.

"So, they don't pass on secret information?"

"Correct," Claire replied. "So, let's get back to my question. Why is Alex lying?"

"Always assuming you're right," Nonie replied. "If he is lying, I think he's trying to protect you."

"From what?"

"From yourself," Nonie revealed. She then thought about what Alex had told her but decided not to divulge her knowledge. Instead, she said, "Alex has realised you suffer from bouts of depression. He is also doing his best to make sure you remain amongst friends. He wants you to be happy. He wants Mick, me and you to remain together as friends."

Claire's mouth opened, but nothing came out.

Nonie said, "Lock the door."

"Why?"

"Do it. We need to talk."

Once Claire had done as instructed, Nonie threw some of the bedclothes back, "Take your shoes off and get in."

"You've got flu."

"Believe me; it's not flu. I've just been suffering from a bad case of Pushley syndrome."

As Claire slid in beside her, Nonie said, "Let's talk about you. Whatever you tell me will remain between us."

"What d'you want to know?"

"I know that Samantha forced Mick to come to Fort Saunders. I also know that you were his wing woman and that you saved Mick's life," Nonie said. "Mick hasn't told me much more. So, fill me in."

"Samantha sent us both to Arcadia to attack the Great Ones," Claire said. "We then discovered that the Great Ones had invaded Cittavecchia and decided to help. The rest you know."

"That doesn't tell me much," Nonie complained.

"It's not a part of my life I really want to think about," Claire replied. "Both Mick and I nearly died."

Realising she was wasting her time with her present line of questioning, Nonie changed tack. Although Alex had told her a great deal, Nonie still opened with, "How long has Alex been with you?"

"I don't know exactly," Claire replied. "We were paired when I was converted into a monarch. I only know this because Alex told me. But Alex's memory banks aren't complete."

"You said paired," Nonie said. "What's that exactly?"

"Monarchs were created at the time true humanoid droids were not available," Claire replied. "It became common practice to pair a TK5 with each monarch. We survived longer if we had droid as a partner."

"The war was a long time ago. There is a large gap. What happened in between?"

"When Alex and I were captured, we were sold," Claire replied. "We were sold several times. We were useful military hardware. Both Alex and I have been reprogrammed, and mind washed several times."

"So how did you end up working for Samantha?" Claire asked.

"Both Alex and I were captured by Samantha," Claire revealed. "Samantha mind washed me again, but Alex escaped and followed me to Arcadia."

Nonie kissed her, "Sound like you've had a tough life, but you are now amongst friends."

CHAPTER SEVENTEEN
THE HUNT FOR PUSHLEY STARTS

Red Moxstroma, Bryn Rosslyn, Chou Lan, Lascaux Kurgan and Brian and Keith Calvert walked into the living room of the hotel suite, Nonie Tomio glanced upwards, "Are you there, Alex?"

Extending a whisper tube, Alex said, "What is it, Nonie?"

Glancing at Lascaux, Nonie said, "Do you think its sensible to involve Lascaux?"

"New Melbourne is a big city," Alex replied. "If you are going to find Ed Pushley you need feet on the ground,"

"You've made me tell so many lies," Nonie observed, "If Lascaux comes with us, it will probably bring her memories back, and she will say something."

"Stop worrying," Alex replied. "I have been monitoring her conversations with Red, and she can't remember very much. She can't even remember very much about the subsequent conversations you had with her."

He then added, "I have to go. Corporal Tarmy is about to start the briefing."

As Alex pulled way, Tarmy said, "Can you display some images of Ed Pushley please?"

Opening a power bubble, Alex began displaying various images of Pushley. In some, he was wearing a monk's habit. In others, Pushley was wearing olive drab. He was then shown in the clothes he'd stolen. Nonie was relieved to note that the last set of images had been doctored by Alex so that they looked as if Pushley was standing in a car park, stun gun at the ready.

As more and more pictures emerged, Tarmy said, "You will notice that Pushley is not averse to dying his hair."

Tarmy instructed Alex to display a plan view of New Melbourne that had been divided into five segments and each segment colour coded, White, Yellow, Blue, Green and Red.

He then said, "We're going to split into five groups; White group; Brian and Keith Calver, Yellow group, Claire and Alex; Blue group, Nonie and me; Green group, Bryn and Chou; Red group, Red and Lascaux."

"We've only two air-cars," Red objected.

"Once we've dropped you off in the city, Brian, Red and Bryn will hire air-cars," Mick replied. He then began handing out bags.

Red glanced in his carrier-bag, "Number plates?"

"Fake number plates to be exact," Tarmy replied. "One of the contractors I've been dealing with knows someone who'd make them no questions asked. Since the police introduced the new camera surveillance system, the market for them has boomed."

"Why do we need them?"

"I've no doubt some of the things we may have to do will be illegal," Tarmy replied. "There's no point attracting police attention if we don't have to."

"If we locate Pushley what do we do?"

"Hopefully, you will be able to stun him," Tarmy replied. "We then take him back to Awis Oasis. Hopefully, they won't let him escape again."

~*~

Landing his air-car close to the New Pacific Hotel, Mick Tarmy ran his eyes over it.

"Pushley's a snob," Nonie Tomio said. "If he's in town, that's the sort of place he'd stay in."

"Okay," Tarmy said. "Let's go and check it out."

After walking into the hotel lobby, Tarmy produced his old

police badge, briefly flashed it, and then handed over a hard copy image, "We're looking for this man. His name is Ed Pushley."

When the concierge looked uncertain, Tarmy added, "We think he may have been responsible for the death of Arnold De-Hegg."

"Who?"

"He was the owner of the Meran Court Hotel," Tarmy reminded the other man. "He flew his air-car into the recent tornado. We believe someone tampered with the controls."

A glimmer of understanding appeared in the other man's eyes, "Ah! Yes. The Meran Court Hotel. I gather it has a rather unsavoury reputation. Sex workers use it."

"We're investigating a possible murder, Tarmy said, "Ed Pushley is a suspect. If he is staying here, he is probably using an alias."

There was a long pause while the concierge interrogated his system. Eventually, Pushley's face appeared in a power bubble, and Tarmy said, "That's him. Which room is he in?"

"He's already checked out. I'm sorry I can't be of more help officer."

As Tarmy and Nonie went back to the air-car, Tarmy said, "He knows we're after him."

"Of course he does," Nonie replied. "He can read our minds. That means he'll be one jump ahead of us, every time."

"Hmm," Tarmy said. "Maybe we'll have to find another way of tracking him down."

~*~

Alton Mygael's percom buzzed. Realising the call was from Mick Tarmy, Mygael went to power bubble mode, and Tarmy's face appeared inside it. Tarmy wasted no time with small talk, "Pushley's turned up like a bad smell."

"Where?"

"He was seen in New Melbourne,"

"Who saw him?"

After swiftly explaining how Pushley had tried to attack Nonie, Tarmy said, "We have been making enquiries, but so far we've made no progress. We know he was staying at the New Pacific Hotel, but he'd checked out a few standard hours before we tracked him down. He either read our minds or guessed we'd come after him. We need more feet on the ground to locate him, or another means of locating him."

Tarmy added, "Alex suspects that Pushley also killed someone using mind control."

"Have you told the local police?"

"They'd laugh at us," Tarmy replied. "D'you really believed that the local police would believe that Pushley is a spettro, and can use special mental powers to force people into doing things they don't want to do? We need more feet on the ground, or another means of locating him."

"I'd like to help you," Alton Mygael replied. "But I have real problems here at the moment."

"What problems?"

"I thought Klaien had called you and explained."

"She told me that she and Allus Wren prevented you leaving for Arden and that Samantha hadn't been deactivated. She also told me not to call her back because she was in police custody."

"She still is," Mygael replied. "They have also arrested Tam Philips and Mih Valanson. I don't want to press charges for assault, but it hasn't made any difference. The teleport company want to make a safety issue out of this. I've no idea if we will be able to do a deal with the local police and have them released any time soon. If we can't, it looks like a long drawn out period of imprisonment and then waiting for it to go to court."

When Tarmy went quiet, Mygael added, "More worrying, Allus Wren is still in a critical condition. They've put him in a suspension unit. They are scared he could end up like Stert Oryx and spontaneously combust."

"That's bad," Tarmy said. He added, "So what you're telling me is you can't help."

"You could see if Lon Freedon could help you," Mygael replied. "I still have him on a private retainer."

For the first time since the conversation started, Tarmy became more upbeat, "Lon Freedon. I used to work with Lon. He was a good cop."

"I know," Mygael replied. "If you want to succeed, it's not what you know, it who you know. If you give me a couple of hours, I'll contact him, and he'll expect your call. As it's our fault that Pushley escaped, I'll also tell him to bill me for his time, okay?"

Tarmy nodded, "That seems fair, considering the amount the trouble Pushley has already caused us."

~*~

Lon Freedon's percom buzzed. Although he didn't recognise the number, he accepted the call. A moment later, a power bubble opened, and a face appeared inside it. Freedon frowned, "Is that you, Mick? Bloody hell. Have you had a facelift or something?"

"Or something," Tarmy replied. "I was shot a while ago. As part of my treatment, I was given life extension drugs. They had one or two unexpected side effects."

"You look about fifteen years younger than when we worked together," Freedon replied.

"I know," Tarmy replied. "It's a bit disconcerting when I look in the mirror."

After discussing how their careers had diverged over the years, Freedon got down to business, "So what can I do for you?"

"What did Alton tell you?"

"He said you were looking for a guy called Ed Pushley," Freedon replied. "I also gather that you suspect he might have committed a murder, but you don't want to involve the police directly."

"Correct."

Freedon went quiet for a second or two and then said, "We can either do this the easy way or the hard way."

"What is it that makes me think you're going to suggest something illegal?" Tarmy said.

"I presume you've heard the old saying: If you want to succeed, it's not what you know, it who you know."

"Yes," Tarmy replied. "It's one of Alton Mygael's favourite sayings. Where's this leading?"

"On Arcadia, there's a slightly different variant: If you want to succeed, it's not what you know, it's how much you bribe."

"Who are we bribing?"

"Most of New Melbourne has facial recognition cameras. Since they were introduced, street crime is running at a fraction of what it was," Freedon replied. "If you have a decent image of Ed Pushley, I can get a friend of mine to log it on the system."

"I can send you several images," Tarmy replied. "But Pushley's no fool. He'll stay hidden."

"He can't stay hidden forever," Freedon replied. "And when he does come out, we'll ID him very quickly."

"We have photographs of him dressed in all sorts of clothing. He's the master of disguise.

"The facial recognition cameras in New Melbourne are very sophisticated. They can see through most disguises," Freedon replied. "I'm probably telling granny how to suck eggs, but they work by analysing facial features. Growing a beard or a false moustache won't throw them off for long. Once we list his name as a priority, it's no holds barred."

"How much is this going to cost?"

"Alton Mygael is paying," Freedon replied. "Why are you worried?"

~*~

Pushley mind linked with Lascaux but after only a few seconds he decided she was no use to him. Not only had she taken to wearing her protective hat following Tarmy's instructions, but the part of her mind that was still accessible was unstable because he'd stunned her during their last encounter.

He then tried entering Red Moxstroma, Bryn Rosslyn and Chou Lan minds in turn and had the same problem.

With no alternative, he tried Nonie. Within seconds he realised that she'd sensed his presence in her mind and mental doors began slamming in his face. Annoyed, he gave up all pretence at subtlety and applied as much pressure as he could muster.

As her mind yielded slightly, Nonie provided him with confirmation of what he already he suspected. His attempt to recover the money and kill Nonie and Lascaux had stirred up a hornets' nest. If he wasn't careful, he'd be stung to death.

"Is something the matter padrone?" Yalt asked.

"Nothing I can't handle," Pushley assured him and then walked over to the window, chinked the curtain and glanced out. As the apartment they were squatting in was on the fifth floor, the surrounding skies were abuzz with air-cars.

"There is something wrong, isn't there?"

Pushley gave a more honest answer, "I sense danger all around."

"What sort of danger?"

"I'm not sure," Pushley admitted. "I feel as if they are closing in."

He then added, "We need to get off this planet as soon as we can."

The words had barely crossed Pushley's lips before high priest's face appeared in his mind, "We have managed to persuade two people who were booked on the teleport to cancel. We anticipate the slots will be offered to you. If they are, take them. If you miss this opportunity, it could be weeks before I can organise an alternative."

Despite his worries, Pushley half-smiled.

The cleric sensed his demeanour, "Is something amusing you?"

"Understatement usually amuses me," Pushley said. "You said you persuaded two people to cancel their teleport bookings. I'm sure it was more brutal than that."

"It was," the cleric admitted. "I convinced the people concerned that a close relative had suddenly died, and they had to return home."

"Had one of their relatives died?"

"No," the cleric replied. "But as they say on your world, you can't make omelettes without cracking eggs."

"When are we due to teleport?"

"In approximately eight hours," the cleric replied. "All being well, the teleport centre will contact you shortly."

Pushley half-smiled again, "So, that's our teleport organised. What about the diplomatic override cards?"

"My contact will meet you outside the teleport centre," the cleric replied. "His name is Vaz Bryon."

"How will we recognise Bryon?"

The cleric created an image of Bryon in Pushley's mind, and then said, "Don't worry. Bryon knows what you look like and will be looking out for you. He will approach you and give you the cards. Two other matters; you must leave your gun behind. If you take it into the teleport centre, you will be arrested."

"Is that it?" Pushley snapped. "You said there were two other things."

"Ah, Yes! We are picking up vague mental images which indicate that Mick Tarmy's people know you are in New Melbourne, and they have private investigators searching for you."

"Then I'm not leaving the gun behind."

"You will not be in any danger if you follow my instructions," the cleric said.

"These investigators. Who are they?"

"We are not sure yet," The high priest replied. "We will let you have more information if we find out, but you need to play safe. Don't take your gun with you. When you reach the teleport centre, go inside as quickly as possible. As there are security guards and police in the building, it's unlikely you will be attacked once you are inside the centre."

Pushley said, "Thanks for the warning."

"Together we are stronger," the cleric reminded him.

CHAPTER EIGHTEEN
THE HOT TIP

C laire Hyndman's percom chirped. As she had different sounds for different people, she knew it was Mick Tarmy calling.

"We may have a lead," Tarmy informed her. "A couple of days back, we went to the New Pacific Hotel, the place where Pushley was staying. I left a photograph of Pushley with them. One of the desk clerks recognised it and said, he'd given Pushley permission to stay in a friend's apartment."

"Where is it?"

"I'm not telling you," Tarmy replied. "I don't want you trying to take him alone. We'll be with you in five minutes."

Claire said, "I'll have to leave you in the car, Alex. We can't risk you being frazzled by an anti-droid Mannheim."

"Understood," Alex replied. "But I can still be of assistance."

A moment later, one of the captured stun guns appeared suspended from one of Alex's spindly arms, "I can control the air-car and fire through the windows without endangering my circuits."

~*~

"You must get out now," the high priest's mental voice snapped. "Tarmy has your location and is moving in in force. You only have minutes to escape."

Pushley didn't have to be told twice. Grabbing his wallet, percom and the stun pistol he'd found, he snapped, "Come on Yalt we have to get out of here."

Yalt began glancing around, "What about our things, padrone?"

"Leave 'em! We have to get out of here, fast."

Once out of the apartment, Pushley ran toward the lift enclosure and began beating out a tattoo on the call button. By the time that Yalt came puffing up alongside him, the lift arrived, and both men piled in.

As the elevator descended, Yalt said, "Where are we going to go, padrone?"

"I've no idea at the moment," Pushley admitted. "But I'm sure I'll think of something."

Once on the ground floor, Pushley made a dash for the back door and out into a ground-level parking area. Noting someone walking towards a parked air-car, Pushley rushed forwards brandishing his stun gun. Taken by surprise, the man just held his hands up and said, "Don't shoot me please."

"If you do as you're told you won't get shot," Pushley snapped and then ordered Yalt into the back. A sense of déjà vu swept over Yalt. When Pushley had hijacked Toni Felado, it hadn't gone well.

Climbing in Pushley snapped, "Drive."

"Where to?"

"Anywhere ... Get us out of this block fast."

He then said to Yalt, "Duck down, so no one sees us."

Once the air-car had carried them for the best part of a kilometre, Pushley let out a sigh of relief and said, "So where were you going?"

When the man hesitated, Pushley began waving the stun gun around. "I said, where were you going?"

"I've got a small lockup on an industrial park; I was going there."

"Anyone there?"

"No."

"Then take us there," Pushley ordered.

Once the air-car had landed in a bay, Pushley glanced at the roller shutter, and the sign over that said, "Stid Henderson Cleaning Services."

"I presume you're Stid Henderson."

The other man nodded, "You're not going to shoot me, are you?"

"I've told you," Pushley snapped. "If you do as you're told you won't get shot. Now open up and then get back here. If you try to run off, I will shoot you."

Once Henderson had lifted the shutter. Pushley was pleased to note that there was enough room for the air-car to park inside. On his return, Pushley told Henderson to drive the air-car in.

Once the other man had complied, Pushley waved the stun gun at Henderson again and said, "Now close the shutter."

After Henderson had done as instructed, Pushley climbed out of the air-car and glanced around at the cleaning machines, "You haven't got many machines, have you?"

"Most of them are out on hire," Henderson replied defensively. "If they're stored in here, they're not earning money."

Glancing towards the rear of the unit, Pushley noted a small office and comfort area and waved Henderson towards it with his gun. Once inside, Pushley pointed towards a desk and said, "Why don't you sit down?"

As Henderson did as instructed, he said, "What's this all about?"

"All you need to know is that we'll be staying here for a few hours," Pushley replied. "I am expecting a call very shortly. When the call comes through, you will take us back into town."

"Then what?"

"I'll let you go," Pushley promised.

~*~

Tarmy's air-car came into view but didn't land. Instead, it

flashed its lights. Claire instructed her air-car to follow Tarmy and the two set off in convoy. Five minutes later, both air-cars touched down, and Tarmy led the way to the lift enclosure.

Once they were on the fifth floor, they carefully worked their way along a corridor, guns at the ready.

Finding the front door to the flat open, Tarmy let out a curse, "Looks like our bird has already flown."

Tapping the door with one foot, Tarmy went in crouched, gun swivelling as he moved. The others followed him, copying his example. Once he'd been through every room, Tarmy called out, "Looks like I was right, he's escaped again."

Claire became accusative, "If you'd told me where he was, I might have caught him."

"Going in without back up is always a bad idea," Tarmy replied, frostily. "Instead of arguing amongst ourselves, let's start searching this area. He can't have gone far, and he might be on foot."

Once he was back in his air-car, Tarmy instructed the machine to start circling the area around the apartment building. He then put in a call to Lon Freedon. After swiftly telling Freedon where they were, the other man said, "I'll contact my facial recognition friend and ask him if anything has been picked up."

A few minutes later, Freedon called back, "The facial recognition system picked up someone looking like Pushley leaving the flats about five minutes before you arrived."

"Why didn't you tell us this before?"

"There are thousands of cameras dotted around New Melbourne," Freedon growled. "They all feed into a central processing installation. It takes time for the system to process so much data, so there is always a time lag."

Tarmy sighed, "Anything else?"

"We have an image of Pushley pointing a gun at someone and leaving in an air-car," Freedon continued.

"A hijack?"

"Looks that way," Freedon said.

"Number plate?"

"The camera couldn't pick it up," Freedon explained, "It probably had anti-detection plates."

Tarmy thought about the fake plates they had fitted to their air-cars, "Yeah, I believe that's very common in New Melbourne these days; anything else?

"Yeah," Freedon said. "We know the colour and make of the air-car. It was a red Ingermann-Verex X 4."

"Do you know where the X 4 went?" Tarmy said.

"Not yet," Freedon said. "But we should have something for you shortly."

"As soon as you can," Tarmy replied.

"Any problem with me joining in the hunt for Pushley?" Freedon said.

"All assistance gladly accepted," Tarmy replied.

~*~

Pushley said, "Stop doing that."

"Doing what?"

"Clicking your pen," Pushley snapped.

Henderson tossed his pen into a stand and then said, "How long will it be before you get this call."

"Not long now," Pushley predicted. He'd barely spoken before his percom sounded. After accepting the call, a slight smile formed on his face, "Thank you for contacting us. We'll take the slot. See you shortly."

Pushley glanced at Henderson and Yalt, "Come on. We're on our way; we're teleporting in two hours."

He then waved the stun gun under Henderson's nose, "Don't try anything; otherwise, I will stun you."

Fear immediately formed on Henderson's face, "There's no need for that."

Once Henderson had backed the air-car out, Yalt slammed the shutter home and dived in next to Pushley. He gave Henderson approximate co-ordinates for an end destination. Because they had to join an air-circulation route around the city, it was over half an hour before Henderson's air-car arrived at a suitable car park.

As the air-car began circling a parking area close to the teleport centre, Yalt glanced at the stun gun that Pushley was holding and said, "I mind-heard what the High Priest told you."

"And what was that?" Pushley demanded.

Yalt whispered. "You were told to leave the gun behind."

"Don't worry," Pushley whispered back, "I'll ditch it once we've got rid of Henderson."

"You're not going to kill him!"

"No!" Pushley snapped.

Once the air-car had landed, Pushley waved the stun gun at Henderson again, "Get out."

Climbing out, Pushley kept this gun trained on Henderson and said, "My friend doesn't want me to kill you."

"No, please don't."

Pushley smiled, "So I've thought of an alternative."

Pushley grabbed the air-car fob from out of Henderson's hand and opened the boot. He then said, "Get in and lie face downward."

Fearing the gun more than the prospect of enforced confinement, Henderson climbed in with remarkable speed. He then turned to face the floor.

Grabbing an emergency bag, Pushley pulled out a short plastimetal rope and tied Henderson's hands. Once he'd slammed the boot shut, Pushley locked the air-car, tossed the fob into a nearby waste bin and then glanced at Yalt, "I didn't kill him. Happy now?"

When Yalt nodded, Pushley said, "Come on. We haven't much time. Let's get to the teleport centre."

CHAPTER NINETEEN

BACK ON THE TRAIL

Lon Freedon's voice came over the air-car intercom, "The system has picked out a sighting of an Ingermann-Verex X 4 landing at a small workshop unit."

As Freedon read out the co-ordinates, Claire heard Mick Tarmy acknowledge and then tell the entire team to converge on the unit.

Claire spoke to Alex, "What's the betting he'll be tipped off and will move out before we get there."

"In all probability," Alex agreed.

A few seconds later, Lon Freedon's voice confirmed their fears by saying, "There's been another sighting in a public car park." He gave them the new coordinates.

As Mick Tarmy hadn't acknowledged Freedon's message, Claire queried the omission.

"He could be in a blackspot," Freedon replied. "I'll try him again."

"Yeah," Claire replied. "Do that. We don't want Pushley getting away this time."

Alex cut in, "Shall I take you to the new location?"

"Yes," Claire replied. "And go as fast as you can without breaking speed limits."

As her air-car picked up speed, she added, "This could be our chance, Alex. If I can get within shooting distance, I'll be able to take him down."

"If you are going to get close to him, you will have to change your appearance," Alex prompted.

Taking the hint, Claire began thinking about a woman who'd once been part of Ed Pushley's team when he'd worked at Fort Saunders. Her name was Avene Nother, and she and Pushley had been more than just work colleagues; they'd had a short intimate relationship until it had collapsed like most of Pushley's liaisons.

Within a matter of seconds, Claire's face changed to Nother's; then her blonde hair turned jet back. To complete her disguise, she reversed the jacket she was wearing. Partway through the process, she lifted her head slightly, "So, what d'you think?"

As Alex had seen Avene Nother, he said, "It's an excellent likeness, ma'am."

"That's the idea," Claire replied, checking her stun gun, "If I find Pushley, I'll get a lot closer to him if he thinks I'm Avene. In any case, if I do get a crack at Pushley and kill him, I don't want my real face displayed by the police and the media."

While she was undergoing the final changes, Alex said, "This might be useful."

One of his spindly arms appeared from behind the invisibility cloak with a small handgun hanging from one finger.

Taking it from Alex, Claire turned it over in her hands. Like the legendary American Derringer, the gun was small, around 100mm in length.

She said, "I remember this. Mick showed it to me once. This is the gun that Samantha gave Mick when she sent him on the first mission. It's a Mini-Max Five. I thought he'd lost it."

Knowing the miniature gun was a special, Claire clicked it open and transformed it into a razor. She then clicked another button and changed it into a percom. She then said, "Mick stopped using the percom in case Samantha was monitoring us."

"Then don't use the percom," Alex replied. "Having a small gun that is easily hidden may be useful."

After slipping the gun into one of her pockets; she glanced

down and realised they were overflying an open-air public car park.

Claire began glancing around, looking for red air-cars. She let out a mild curse when she realised that there were several red air-cars parked up; red was the in colour.

While she was still staring around, Alex said, "There is a red Ingermann-Verex X 4 over there, and its engine is still warm."

Claire yelped, "Put me down near to it, fast."

As Claire's air-car touched down, she leapt out and raced towards the other car, stun gun drawn. While she was staring into the locked vehicle, she heard a muffled cry from the boot and ran around to the back.

While she was trying to force the boot open, her air-car came drifting towards her with one of the windows ajar. One of Alex's skinny arms was projecting out holding a fob. "This had been dumped in a litter bin."

Grabbing it from him, Claire opened the boot.

Stid Henderson blinked owlishly, and the said, "Thank God. I thought I'd be in here for hours."

He then shouted, "Can you untie me please."

As Claire began undoing the knots, she said, "I suppose it's a daft question, but do you know where the guy that tied you up went?"

"There are two of 'em," Henderson replied. "A big guy that did all the talking and a weedy guy who just seemed to do what he was told."

"Are you sure there were two of them?"

"Sure, I'm sure," Henderson said, "I heard the big guy tell the little one that they were going to the teleport centre,"

He climbed out of the boot and reclaimed his fob.

"Where is the teleport centre?" Claire demanded.

Gaining his bearings, Henderson pointed towards a large building about four hundred meters away. "That's it, over there."

When Claire called out to Alex, Henderson said, "If you're going after them. You'd be better on foot. The piazza and side streets adjoining the teleport centre is Mannheim protected. No air-cars allowed."

Realising she couldn't take Alex with her, she began running. Half turning, she called out, "Tell Mick and the others that I'm going after Pushley. And make sure they know I'm in disguise. Take a photograph of me. I don't want them shooting me by mistake."

~*~

"I hope to God this contact turns up," Pushley griped and began glancing around the crowded concourse, searching for a would-be attacker. His fears suddenly evaporated as he caught a glimpse of Vaz Bryon. Almost instantaneously, a look of recognition crossed the other man's face, and he turned towards them.

Being at least two metres in height and well built, Bryon swiftly ploughed his way through the seething crowds with the efficiency of an icebreaker slicing through pack-ice. After giving Pushley a swift handshake, Bryon slipped the diplomatic override cards into Pushley's top pocket and said, "You must keep the cards with you at all times."

He then handed Pushley their boarding cards, "You'll need these. Don't lose them."

The high priest sent Pushley a mental message, "You must go now. If you stay here, your enemies may try to kill you."

The cleric then supplied Pushley with an image of Claire Hyndman in her Avene Nother disguise and said, "This is the person Tarmy's sent after you."

"But I know that woman." Pushley mentally protested. "Avene Nother wouldn't harm me...."

"She is not what she seems," the cleric replied. "She is the one you call Claire Hyndman in disguise."

"Hyndman? The monarch?"

"Correct," the high priest said. "She has changed her appearance and looks like Avene Nother. I think she's hoping she can lure you into a trap. I can't read her mind, but I am picking up the thoughts of others which suggest she is armed and hopes to kill you. She's definitely coming your way. She found Stid Henderson locked in the boot of his car. He's told him you are going to teleport centre."

Pushley suddenly hit flashpoint; after being chased across the city, his fears changed to anger, "Hyndman after me? So, she wants to kill me, eh! Not if I kill her first!"

"I know you dislike Claire Hyndman," the cleric said. "But you must not let that cloud your judgement. She is dangerous. You need to leave now."

Instead of doing as instructed, Pushley pulled out his stun gun began glancing around again, "If Tarmy's bitch is around here, I'll kill her."

Bryon reacted swiftly, grabbed hold of Pushley's gun and wrenching it out his grasp. Slipping the stun gun into one of his own pockets, Bryon hissed, "Are you mad! You'll get us arrested if you start waving a weapon around in a public space."

He then took hold of one of Pushley's shoulders and dragged him towards the main entrance doors. Partway there, Bryon said, "Forget the woman," shoved Pushley through the door and snapped, "You must go. Now!"

Knowing he didn't have time to impose his will on Bryon and was no match for him in a fight, Pushley caved in, "Okay! You win!"

Leaving Pushley, Bryon walked over to Yalt and said, "Your mate is in danger. Whatever you do, don't let him come back out here under any circumstances."

Picking up on the urgency, Yalt went racing after Pushley. Once he'd caught his boss up, Yalt said, "You mustn't go back, padrone."

"So everyone keeps telling me," Pushley growled.

The high priest's image came into Pushley's mind almost immediately, "You would be wise to heed caution. The danger is very real. Now go! You are early, but there is a waiting room in the teleport centre. Go there now! Claire Hyndman doesn't have boarding cards, so the security guards won't allow her to follow you."

Glancing back, Pushley noted that Bryon was still standing by the main doors to make sure he didn't change his mind.

"We're on our way," Pushley replied.

"Good," the cleric said. "I suggest you use the stolen IDs you have for now but keep your diplomatic override cards with you at all times."

As Pushley led the way deeper into the teleport complex, Yalt looked worried, "This is a huge place, padrone."

"It's no different than the teleport centre you worked in at Awis Oasis Yalt," Pushley replied. "It just has more teleport bays."

When Yalt took a deep breath and held it, Pushley said, "Is there something the matter, Yalt?"

"I'm trained in teleportation, and I've seen people teleport," Yalt replied. "Many people, padrone. But I have never done it myself."

Pushley shrugged, "It's virtually painless, nothing to worry about."

He added, "So take that hangdog look off your face, Yalt. It'll attract attention."

Once Yalt had forced a smile, Pushley walked towards a checkpoint. While still in the queue, he began working on the guard's mind. Arriving, he presented, the boarding passes and Ben Ellis's ID and pointed at Yalt. He then showed Toni Felado's ID and indicated the ID was his. A few seconds later, they were both waved through.

Once on the other side of the barrier, Pushley let out a sigh of relief. If the high priest was telling the truth, Claire Hyndman couldn't catch him now. Glancing up at an electronic notice board, he began studying their teleport journey.

As New Victoria was an illegal colony, the teleport centre in New Melbourne could only link with two other centres, one was on Arden, and the other was SS5, a privately financed non-aligned Space Station in orbit around Arcadia.

After studying the electronic board for some time, Pushley realised that once they'd cleared Arden or SS5, they'd then be shunted through twenty-four other teleport centres before they arrived on Midway.

Noting his observations, Yalt said, "It is a long way padrone. We will need a long rest when we arrive. Otherwise, we may end up like Stert Oryx and his men."

Pushley gave him a sharp look, "How d'you knows about Stert Oryx?"

"The high priest told me," Yalt said.

Annoyed the high priest kept on mind linking with Yalt, Pushley said, "And what else did the meddlesome cleric say?"

"He said I have to make sure you did not endanger your life unnecessarily," Yalt replied.

"And why would I do that?"

"I do not know padrone," Yalt said. "I am only telling you what the high priest told me."

"Well, don't worry," Pushley assured him. "I don't intend to take any risks."

Once they'd entered the waiting room, Pushley selected a corner location and then let his mind wander. Within seconds he'd mind linked with Bryon who was still lurking around near the main entrance.

Concerned that Claire Hyndman might be able to circum-navigate security and attack him, Pushley began working on Bryon's mind but to little avail. The more he tried, the more that Bryon resisted. But then, Pushley's mental battering ram forced its way through. As the initial breach widened, Pushley sensed his victim's surprise. Once he was confident that Bryon was no longer resisting, Pushley gave him new orders. "You have my gun. If you see Claire Hyndman, you will kill her."

He then sent Bryon a mental image of Claire Hyndman in her Avene Nother disguise.

~*~

When Claire arrived, one of the departure boards was flashing. Although she had no proof, she sensed that Pushley was about to escape and began moving towards the entrance doors, but she never reached them because her legs suddenly gave way and the hard surface of the concourse seemed to leap up at her.

As she slid along the terrazzo paving, she realised she wasn't alone. The whole area seemed to be filled with writhing bodies. After sliding two or three metres, scraping the skin from her elbows in the process, Claire ended up face-to-face with a man. Winded, she still gasped, "What happened?"

"I'm not sure," the man replied and ran a hand over one of his legs. "I think we've been partially stunned."

The stranger then caught a glimpse of Bryon picking his way through the pile of bodies. As Byron was brandishing Pushley's stun pistol, the stranger realised what had happened, "That gun-happy creep over there has fired a low sweep over the whole concourse and has taken our legs out, that's what's happened."

"Why would he do that?"

Glancing up and noting that Bryon was picking his way through the mass of bodies, the stranger said, "He's a hitman. He's obviously after someone. He took everyone down to make life easy for himself."

Producing a stun gun, the stranger swivelled slightly and then issued a challenge. Instead of heeding the verbal warning, Bryon turned towards his voice and fired first. Taking a hit, the stranger dropped his gun. Realising she was in danger; Claire began searching frantically in her pockets for her own stun gun but realised she was lying on it and the deadweight of her partially stunned body made it inaccessible.

Her movements attracted Bryon's attention. He was closing the distance between them, a lob-sided smile formed on his face. He said, "Well! Well! Well! If it isn't Tarmy's bitch."

Being unable to pull her own stun gun, she thought about the Mini-Max Five that Alex had just given her. Claire then heard distinct clicks as Bryon selected kill mode. He then took careful aim. "Time to die, Tarmy's bitch."

Realising he was about to kill her, Claire managed to roll sideways dodging the first shot; locating the Mini-Max mid-roll, she twisted again and then fired back three times in quick succession.

When Bryon just staggered and levelled his gun at her again, Claire realised the Mini-Max was set on minimum stun; she flipped the setting with her thumb and fired once more. This time Bryon spasmed as if he'd been struck by lightning and then collapsed across two of his victims.

A moment later, two uniformed police officers, appeared weapons drawn. The stranger hissed, "Put the gun away. Now!"

Realising the two police officers might assume she was the gunman and might shoot first and ask questions later, Claire did as instructed. She'd barely secreted her weapon before one of the uniforms came over and glanced down at the stranger, "Is that Lon?"

"Yeah."

"You okay, Lon?"

Lon nodded and then pointed at Bryon, "He's the perp that shot everyone. Check him out."

As the uniformed officer walked away, Claire said, "So you're Lon Freedon?"

"That's me."

"How come you are so pally with the local police?"

"I've done 'em a few favours in the past," Freedon replied. "I've also contributed towards the local police fund."

"Given out a few bribes, you mean?"

"That's a harsh assessment of the situation," Freedon replied.

While they were still talking, one of the uniformed officers checked Bryon's pulse. He then began rifling Bryon's pockets. Finding Bryon's ID, the officer called out his name's and then glanced back at Lon shaking his head, "Dead as a doornail. Did you take him down?"

Lon Freedon nodded, "I had no choice. He was going to fire again."

Once the uniform had moved off, Claire's tone became acid, "Do you always claim other people's kills?"

"Believe it or not, I've just done you a big favour," Lon replied. "You discharged a weapon in a public place, and I suspect you don't have a license to carry. But I'll stick with my story and say I shot Bryon. I do have a licence to carry."

"That's appreciated," Claire said. She then glanced at an electronic notice board and swore, "Pushley is going to escape."

~*~

As Bryon died, Pushley uttered an oath; Claire Hyndman had managed to survive. Yalt gave him a worried look, "Is there something wrong, padrone?"

Instead of answering, Pushley glanced at the wall clock and cursed again; going after Claire Hyndman was now out of the question; his teleport was less than five minutes away. Besides, as he no longer had a gun and the external concourse was crawling with police, he'd end up being arrested if he went back and attempted to kill her.

While he was still mentally fuming, Yalt gave him a nudge, "Time to go, padrone."

Two minutes later, they both disappeared into the ether.

~*~

"Are you okay, Toni?"

Slight pause; "Are you okay, Toni?"

On the second time of asking, Ed Pushley reacted to his alias, "Yes. But I feel drained."

"That's not surprising," the pedestal droid said.

Pushley turned his head slightly and eyed the machine thoughtfully. As he'd lived on Arcadia for several years, a place where droids were banned, he was unused to being surrounded by automatons like the one standing next to him.

The droid in question comprised a wide-based floor-mounted traction unit, a thin shiny stem that led towards a bulky body and vaguely human-looking head unit. Partway up, the machine had spindly flexible arms and three-fingered hands.

Hints of femininity were provided by a soft voice, a pink nurse's hat and a long pink plastimetal skirt that partially covered the body and the stem.

The droid said, "Can I get you anything, Toni?"

When Pushley just shook his head but didn't say anything, the pedestal droid interpreted his body language and said, "I'm not surprised that you're tired, Toni. Both you and Ben have passed through twenty-four teleport gates to get here."

When Pushley still made no effort to engage, the droid added, "My name is Anna. I will be looking after you while you are with us."

Pushley finally broke his silence, "Are we on Midway?"

"You certainly are," Anna replied.

"What time is it?"

When Anna told him, Pushley frowned disbelievingly.

Interpreting the reaction, Anne said, "Some people think teleportation is instantaneous like they see on the movies. But as I said, you passed through twenty-four teleport gates to get here. There are electronic transfer stations on each gate, and there are always delays passing through each one."

Pushley said, "Right."

In an attempt to keep him engaged, Anna baited a hook, "Would you like something to eat or drink, Toni?"

This time, Pushley nodded, "Okay. Yes, please, Anna."

Once he'd been served, Pushley glanced around, and used Yalt's alias, "Where's Ben?"

Anna smiled and pulled back a curtain. Yalt was lying on an adjacent bed, and another nursing droid was fussing around him; he looked as if he was enjoying the attention.

Giving him a slight smile of recognition, Yalt said, "Hello, padrone." Then, remembering Pushley's alias, he said, "Hello, padrone Toni."

"Hello, Ben," Pushley replied. He glanced at Anna, "So when do we get out of here?"

"You seem to be in a rush to leave us, Toni," Anna scolded. "You need to stay in recovery for at least eight hours, maybe longer. Your body is still unstable."

Pushley recalled what had happened to Stert Oryx and his henchmen. They had been warned that their bodies were unstable, but fired by greed, they'd ignored the warnings and had pushed on regardless. Pushley thought about Oryx's fiery end. Oryx and his men had become involved in a firefight. When they were hit, instead of just being injured, their unstable bodies had disintegrated. They'd literally burst into flames.

Anne said, "If you don't stay in recovery for several hours and then take it easy when you are released ..."

"... I could spontaneously combust," Pushley finished, "Nothing left of me other than a pile of ash. "

"If you do as you are told," Anna said, "That won't happen. If you don't do as you're told that may happen. "

"After we've been through recovery, we can go?"

"No!" Anna replied sharply. "Once you have recovered, you will be transferred to the quarantine unit as per the pre-teleport notes."

"Pre-teleport notes. What are they?"

"You obviously didn't read your pre-teleport notes," Anna admonished. "Everyone coming from other system locations to Midway has to submit to quarantine. The rules are designed to prevent diseases from being transferred from colony to colony via the teleport."

"How long does quarantine take?"

"It's a month minimum, but it usually takes around six weeks," Anna replied.

"Six weeks!" Pushley shrieked, "I have important things to do."

"You will be allowed to communicate with your Midwain friends and clients by percom and major computer networks, but you will not be permitted to leave quarantine until signed off by our doctors."

When Pushley swore out loud, Anna said, "Can I remind you,

abusing medical staff, even droids, is a criminal offence."

Realising he was digging a hole for himself, Pushley back-tracked. "No offence meant, Anna. I apologise."

"Apology accepted."

"Thank you."

Anna's mouth opened slightly to expose a set of artificial teeth, the droid equivalent of a smile, "You are stressed, Toni. I am programmed to understand human frailties."

Encouraged by the comments, Pushley said, "I am sure if I had my percom, my stress levels would fall."

Anna gave him another droid smile and then came back with the device. Once the nursing droids had left the room to attend to other teleportees, Pushley finished off his food and drink and then picked up his percom and turned it on. He then began searching for news reports coming out of New Melbourne.

Within seconds he found several news channels talking about a mass shooting in the concourse outside the teleport centre. He then saw images of a woman sprinting towards the teleport concourse. Although she looked like Avene Nother, Pushley knew it was Claire Hyndman in disguise.

Noting the intense look on Pushley's face, Yalt said, "What are you doing, padrone?"

"Thinking and planning my next move," Pushley replied.

Once he'd run and re-run the news reports, Pushley began flicking through his files again. Glancing over, Yalt caught a glimpse of the screen and smiled, "Are you being Agent Q449 again?"

When Pushley nodded, Yalt said, "What is your next move, padrone?"

"Shush," Pushley replied, "I'm thinking," and began going through the electronic correspondence he'd sent from his fake account.

As Pushley continued to re-read the poison he'd been drip-feeding to the authorities, a grin formed on his face. Simple logic dictated; if he threw enough mud in Tarmy's direction, some of it was bound to stick.

While Pushley was still reading, he out a whoop of delight.

Sensing that Pushley had just received good news, Yalt said, "You seem pleased all of a sudden, padrone."

"That's because one of my contacts has just informed me that Targon Yatboon has been arrested," Pushley replied.

"Who's Targon Yatboon?"

Pushley said, "I've good reason to believe the reason why Mick Tarmy came to Awis Oasis was to obtain false IDs from Targon Yatboon. By changing his ID, Tarmy would no longer have to fear being arrested as a war criminal. The same goes for Claire Hyndman. With a new ID, she would no longer be a wanted monarch."

"I do not understand," Yalt said.

"Now that Targon Yatboon has been arrested, Tarmy will be in real trouble," Pushley explained. "His ID will be worthless. His goose will be well and truly cooked."

"Eh!" Yalt said. "What goose?"

"It's an idiom," Pushley replied. He added, "A saying."

"I still don't know what you mean," Yalt replied.

Pushley let out a sigh. "At times, Yalt, you can be hard work. Forget the goose. Now that Targon Yatboon has been arrested, Tarmy's house of cards will collapse. With all the files I sent in as Agent Q449 and the copies sent to the local police, and the local media, it will only be a matter of time before people start asking questions. Once they do, Mick Tarmy and Claire Hyndman will be in real trouble."

He tapped his percom. "All my files are all in here, and when I have completed my next report, I'm going to attach them again. Now that Claire Hyndman has become involved in a killing, the police will be forced into investigating everything."

When Yalt didn't react. Pushley said, "Here's another saying for you, revenge is a dish best served cold."

"I don't understand," Yalt replied.

After doing his best to explain, Pushley let out a contented sigh, "All you need to know is everything is coming together now, Yalt. Very shortly, Mick Tarmy and his friends will rue the day our paths crossed."

"I hope the high priest knows what you are doing," Yalt said.

As if by magic, at the mention of his name, the high priest's face appeared in Pushley's mind.

The cleric gave him a smile and said, "The teleport went well then."

Pushley sent the cleric a mental message back, "It did, but unfortunately, we're going into quarantine for several weeks."

"I'm sure there will be a way around that," the high priest replied brightly.

"What way?" Pushley demanded. "I'm surrounded by droids. You've said it yourself; we can't use our metal skills against droids. A droid's mind doesn't work in the same way as a human mind does."

"I'm sure we'll find a way around the problem," the high priest cooed. "But if we can't you will just have to sit out your quarantine period; in the meantime, I'm sure that you can occupy your time productively. Your first task is to secure us a mobile teleport to replace the one that was lost when Tarmy's people attacked Cittavecchia. You will also need a teleport for your side of the operation."

"I thought you wanted me to find a suitable warehouse," Pushley queried.

"Until you leave quarantine, that will not be possible, will it?" the cleric replied. "You really must learn to be patient."

"Be patient!" Pushley mind screamed, "Six weeks is a long time. What if the Midwain authorities discover we're travelling on bogus documents and arrest us before we get out of here?"

"That is unlikely, because your diplomatic cards will protect you," The high priest replied. Once the cleric's mind link had faded again, Pushley went into the top pocket of his jacket and checked the diplomatic override card he'd been given by Bryon.

As a small green LED in one corner was still glowing, Pushley assumed it was working correctly and returned it to his pocket. He climbed out of bed and staggered towards the nearest window. Once he'd glanced out, his mood changed and he out a sniff of disapproval.

Yalt asked, "Is there a problem, padrone?"

"Other than the fact that the only view out of the window appears to be the rubbish bins," Pushley growled. "And, we are likely to be incarcerated in quarantine for six weeks, everything is just fine."

Going back to his percom, Pushley began tapping again. After the best part of twenty minutes, he stopped, and a very self-satisfied look formed on his face. Tarmy's life was about to become very unpleasant.

Once the message had gone, Pushley recalled his conversation with the high priest and began checking out sites on Midway which could supply and export portable teleport systems.

After trawling through a list of names, Pushley noted suitable contacts and began making a series of calls, "Hi, I'm wondering if you sell portable teleport systems?"

~*~

Don Hagood's percom sounded. As he had his call tones programmed, he knew it was his boss calling, "Yes, sir?"

"Have you heard about the shooting in the teleport concourse, Detective Inspector?"

"No, sir."

"Lon Freedon's involved."

"Freedon?"

"It's all yours. Make sure you nail him."

Hagood grinned, "Payback time, eh!"

"Exactly. There is also a woman called Claire Hyndman involved. You might be interested in looking into to look at her files."

THE AUTHOR

By day mild mannered Andrew R. Williams is a chartered surveyor.... but after twilight falls, he snatches up his pen and lets the writing take control. The Arcadia's Children series are sci-fi thrillers which pour out of Andrew on only the coldest and darkest of nights. When he isn't writing, or chartered surveying, Andrew spends time with his wife Geraldine, staring up at the stars, and plotting eventual world domination. Don't let that calm demeanour and easy smile fool you, oh no.

Other Books By Andrew R Williams:

Science Fiction
Arcadia's Children (Samantha's Revenge)
ISBN 978-1- 61309-710-6 (also in ebook)

Arcadia's Children 2: The Fyfield Plantation
ISBN 978-1- 61309-630-7 (also in ebook)

Novel (Action Thriller)
Jim's Revenge: ISBN ISBN-10: 1916312411
ISBN-13: 978-1916312418

Technical Books

Technical Domestic Building Surveys
ISBN 0 419 178000 7 (also in ebook)

Spons Practical Guide to Alterations and Extension
ISBN 10: 0-415-43426-2 (also in ebook)

Web Links:
https://www.amazon.co.uk/Andrew-R.-Williams/e/
B001HPK7KK

https://www.arcadiaschildren.com/

http://www.authorsden.com/andrewrwilliams

REVIEWS

Arcadia's Children: Samantha's Revenge

5.0 out of 5 stars Beautifully written

Shape-shifting mind-bending thriller that kept me hooked from the first chapter. Williams is now one of my favourite up-and-coming fantasy/science fiction authors, and I'll avidly await his future releases. The characters were fully developed, which is something you don't always find with smaller press publishing house authors. I would definitely recommend giving this a read for any fans of the sci-fi/fantasy genres.

I usually don't enjoy sci-fi books, but I thought I would give this a read. Which I am delighted I did, the price of the book is reasonable for the amount to read and the quality you are given. I definitely recommend 5/5 stars

Arcadia's Children 2: The Fyfield Plantation

Jewel
5.0 out of 5 stars I highly recommend

Did it again!! Great Book, I must say. The way the story unfolds and take you deep into another world is simply fantastic;

Andrew's writing is awe-inspiring. I loved the mindset of Mick Tarmy and the way he handled every scenario; basically, I loved how the author portrayed it. The way the situations were explained was so impressive. I did not even want to take a break from it. I just wanted to fall into the story more and more. I found Tarmy's priorities and his affection to his daughter and his little group quite endearing. I highly recommend this book to all readers who enjoy stories about other worlds like me.

Piaras
5.0 out of 5 stars Another well-crafted sci-fi fantasy sequel.

Author Andrew R. Williams weaves another fantastic sci-fi fantasy with intriguing twists and turns that will easily captivate the reader's attention from the opening page. The author paints an exciting and adventurous story of aliens, robots and clones in a very vivid and convincing way. The characters are drawn with great credibility and integrity.

Jim's Revenge

5.0 out of 5 stars A perfect build-up to a hilarious ending

Jim's Revenge is completely different from Andrew William's other novels so I must admit, I read it wondering whether he could deliver the same quality. The answer is definitely. The characters are well drawn and the plot is as intense as always - leading to an ending that is hilarious as well as action packed. How Williams manages to pull all the threads of his plot together is beyond me, but yet again he has triumphed. A definite must-read.

Printed in Great Britain
by Amazon

39332559R00119